W9-BSM-614

I AM FARTACUS

CHECK OUT THESE OTHER ALADDIN MAX BOOKS!

The Last Boy at St. Edith's

33 Minutes

Under Locker and Key

COMING SOON:

The Wild Bunch

I AM FARTACUS

MARK MACIEJEWSKI

ALADDIN
NEW YORK LONDON TORONTO SYDNEY NEW DELHI

This book is a work of fiction. Any references to historical events, real people, or real places are used fictitiously. Other names, characters, places, and events are products of the author's imagination, and any resemblance to actual events or places or persons, living or dead, is entirely coincidental.

ALADDIN
An imprint of Simon & Schuster Children's Publishing Division
1230 Avenue of the Americas, New York, New York 10020
First Aladdin hardcover edition April 2017

Also available in an Aladdin MAX paperback edition.

Book designed by Laura Lyn DiSiena
The text of this book was set in Janson.
Manufactured in the United States of America 0317 FFG
10 9 8 7 6 5 4 3 2 1
This book has been cataloged with the Library of Congress.
ISBN 978-1-4814-6420-8 (hc)
ISBN 978-1-4814-6419-2 (pbk)
ISBN 978-1-4814-6421-5 (eBook)

This book is dedicated to the Papercuts: Angie, Cindy, David, Donna, Jason, and Kayla.

Let's not get all sappy about it.

CHAPTER 1

Once, in front of pretty much the whole school, Moby cut a fart so loud it sounded like a phone book being ripped in half.

I was there. It changed my life.

Moby never even acknowledged it. He just walked away like nothing happened, but the rest of us who weren't already dying of laughter were left to perish from cheddar-flavored colon-gas poisoning. Cutting a gigantic fart in a crowded cafeteria is the kind of thing that can change your whole destiny, but Moby couldn't have cared less. I knew right then we'd be best friends.

My name is Maciek Trzebiatowski. Don't worry,

you don't need to remember how to spell it. It's pronounced "Maw-check Chub-a-tess-key," but people call me Chub because that's the sound "Trzeb" makes in Polish. With a name like that, I know there's no chance I'll ever be one of the popular kids, but don't lose any sleep. I'm over it.

Moby and I don't want to be popular anyway. As far as I can tell, popularity doesn't mean much of anything outside the walls of school. What Moby and I want is to show everyone that the popular kid isn't everything he seems to be.

If we end up becoming infamous in the process, I guess that's a form of popularity I wouldn't mind.

I know what you're asking yourself. Why bother? Why not just blend in like all the rest of the unpopular kids until one day you become the popular kid's boss?

Why? Because when you are a bald sixth grader with a little bit of a Polish accent, blending in isn't an option. When you throw in the fact that the guy who used to be my best friend is now the king of the popular crowd and won't even admit he knows me—let's just say I have my reasons.

Who is this jerk? You know the kid everyone treats like a superhero. He goes to your school; he goes to *every* school. He is a foot taller than everyone by fifth grade. His name is usually Steve or Troy, always one syllable for some reason. At my school his name is Archer Norris, but a couple of years ago, when he became the star of the basketball team, he started calling himself the Arch, and it stuck. When you're *that* kid, the things you say and do don't have to make sense; kids will copy you, just hoping some of your popularity will rub off on them. It's sad, but you know it's true.

Anyway, just because these freaks are taller, better-looking, and more athletic and have hair (more on that later) doesn't mean they should be the only ones who get to say how life works in middle school. The fact that their bodies have no sense of timing doesn't mean they're the superheroes everyone makes them out to be, which is where Moby and I come in. Every hero needs a villain, so we've made it our business to expose the Arch as the ordinary sixth-grade mortal that I know he is. And I'm here to tell you, business is booming.

Batman once said something like, "Light is defined by the shadow it casts." Archer "the Arch" Norris is the sun at the center of the Alanmoore Middle School solar system; Moby and me, we're the shadows.

School is back in session after spring break. I use the back door by the Dumpsters so I can hit the back stairs instead of using the crowded main hallway. The hallway is torture for me, and I avoid it at all costs. It's difficult for people to pick on you in front of a teacher during class. But in the hallway it's the law of the jungle. In the halls popular kids are like pumas, and I'm like a sloth with asthma and a limp. Something is always trying to take a bite out of my butt.

The stone halls of the ancient building are chilly after sitting empty for a week, and the fumes from cleaning chemicals burn my eyes. Apparently, our janitor, Mr. Kraley, didn't get the week off like we did. The place might look like an old asylum, but it smells new. I bet the smell makes most people think of clean places. The smell of chemicals just makes me miss my hair.

Everyone is buzzing after a week off school. I have to turn sideways to slide past a clump of giggling girls.

One of them says "Hawaii" and I try not to think about the five days I just spent at my parents' dry cleaning shop while my classmates were apparently jetting around the globe. I worked on my "character" while they worked on their tans.

A group of guys from the track team are gathered on the landing. I could turn around and take the long way to my locker, but they are so distracted high-fiving one another, I can probably slide past unnoticed. I flip up the hood of my sweatshirt, turtle my head as low as I can on my shoulders, and try to sneak by without any comments.

I'm safely by them when one whips my hood off my head.

"Look, it's Yoda!" he says.

"Bald, he is," another one chimes in. The rest of the jocks crack up, even though he sounds more like Miss Piggy than Yoda.

I want to explain to them that Yoda is actually a Jedi Master and could easily destroy all of them before they even knew what happened, but something tells me that would only make things worse. So I keep walking.

Me and Moby's lockers are in a bricked-up, dead-end hallway that used to be part of an old stairwell leading from the basement to the library about a hundred years ago. It's a nice spot because it keeps us out of the main hallway. I quickly scan the area to make sure no one sees what I keep in my locker, then I open it and dig through my stack of supplies.

I save anything and everything I can possibly use in a future plot to embarrass the Arch. I haven't pulled a prank against him since I propped a gallon of expired milk against the inside of his locker door two weeks ago, and I'm dying to get back to work. I still have a few copies of the eighth-grade health class childbirth video *Wondrous Womb from Whence We Came*. I swapped one for the sixth-grade *Grammar Is Groovy* DVD. Most people wouldn't guess that someone as cool as the Arch faints at the mere sound of the word "biology," but it's true. I was hoping he'd watch the video by accident and pass out. Unfortunately, he was home sick the day the class sat down to learn the proper use of semicolons or whatever and got to witness the miracle of birth instead. A couple of the boys, including a few jocks, cried a little. But without Archer fainting, I couldn't call that particular prank a success. I consider running the videos over to Ms. Harper's room for another try, but I seriously doubt I could get away with it twice. Nothing else catches my eye.

Moby arrives and digs in his locker a few doors down from mine. It looks like he's searching for books, but I know he's just trying to avoid eye contact with other students.

"You want to come over and finish *Watchmen* tonight?" I ask.

Moby has to read the *good* comics at my house because his parents think they'll turn him into a drooling murderer.

Moby shuts his locker, shoulders his enormous backpack, and sighs. "I can't."

"But you only have, like, fifty pages left!"

His shoulders slump. "I got TD tonight."

Moby's grandfather lives with them. He's a retired army colonel and believes in keeping a tight personal grooming schedule. The Colonel is pretty cool—he unwittingly gives us many of our best ideas for messing with the Arch. The only problem is he can't bend down and reach his own feet to trim his toenails, so Moby has to do it for him. As the lowest-ranking member of the Dick family, Moby draws toenail detail once a month. He spends a lot of time praying his parents will have another child so he can get out of it.

"Has it been a month already?" I ask.

He doesn't answer. He doesn't have to. He shudders like a dog that's about to throw up, and I change the subject.

"Jarek was over last night," I say.

He perks up a bit. "Did they get a new movie?"

My cousin Jarek runs the local movie theater, the Clairemont—an ancient movie house that still uses old-fashioned film projectors.

"One came in yesterday. He'll have it spliced and ready for us to watch it Wednesday after school."

"It's not another classic, is it?"

Ever since I convinced him to watch *Spartacus* last summer, he gets suspicious when he doesn't know what the new movie is.

"Don't worry, new release."

He turns to me, his eyes burning the side of my face. "I hope so. *Spartacus* didn't make any sense."

I'm tired of trying to explain the famous scene where all the slaves claim to be Spartacus so the Romans can't tell which one really is.

Moby won't let it go. "I mean, seriously, how can they *all* be Spartacus? That's a pretty big mess-up, if you ask me."

"Mmm-hmm," I say, hoping he'll drop it.

He doesn't. "And if there's more than one, shouldn't the movie be called *Sparta-CI*?" He taps his temple. "Think about it."

I don't need to think about it. "Don't worry, I promise this one is not a classic."

"Is it age appropriate?"

"I think it's about owls trying to save the world or something."

"Sounds lame, but my parents should be okay with it." Moby's parents make sure the movies he watches are "age appropriate," which seriously limits our options.

Moby shuts his locker and grabs my arm. "Wait! Did they get it?"

I shake my head. The "it" he's asking about is the first trailer for the new *League of Honor* movie that's coming out this summer. We've already decided it's our favorite movie of all time, despite the fact that nobody has even seen a single frame of the film yet. Jarek has promised to tell me the second it arrives.

Just thinking about *League of Honor* appears to wipe the Colonel's ancient, yellow toenails from his mind. He doesn't smile exactly, but I know it lifted his spirits.

Jarek has to watch every film before showing it to a real audience to make sure he's put the film strips together right. We get to watch the movies the day before they're released. I would probably eat a bag of hair to see movies before they are released. There's something supercool about knowing things nobody else knows.

We're about to start planning snacks for our latest private premiere when we hear Shelby behind us.

"What's happening Wednesday after school?" Shelby Larkin asks. Her voice stops us cold.

We've been here too long and she's found us. I glance at Moby without turning around. His eyes plead with me.

"Nothing, Shelby. Moby is gonna come over and read the last fifty pages of *Watchmen*." I try to look busy in my locker.

"Hmm. Will that be before or after you watch the new movie at the Clairemont?"

My scalp flushes. I shut my locker and turn to face her.

If someone figured out how to genetically splice an eleven-year-old girl with a flamingo, Shelby would be the result. All her clothes are from thrift stores and smell like funeral parlors and old perfume. Today she has a sweater buttoned around her neck, but her arms aren't in the sleeves. Shelby has been trying to get invited to the theater since she found out about our deal last year. So far Moby and I have been able to fend her off. I have no idea why she wants to hang out with us anyway—it's not like I've ever been nice to her.

She pushes her glasses up her nose and leans down

so we're eye to eye. I try not to blink as she peers into my soul.

After a moment of the human-lie-detector routine she is satisfied that I'm lying and straightens up. "Uh-huh, that's what I thought." She folds her arms and stares some more.

I tell myself not to sweat as her bird eyes bore into me, but it's no good. Beads form on my bare head. I have to get away before some roll down into my eye. I'm an awful liar and it shows.

I start to say, "Let's go, Mo—" But when I turn, Moby is gone. He knows if we stick around, Shelby will eventually get the truth. After that, how long before we give in and let her come with us to a screening? Moby has slipped away, leaving me to deal with the flamingo.

Well played, kid.

I'm about to suggest she earn her ticket to the screening by trimming the Colonel's toenails when the intercom crackles. An earsplitting squeal is followed by the voice of our principal.

"Good moooorning, Alanmoore students. This is

Mr. Mayer." The intercom is ancient like the school, so kids move closer to hear. I know a chance to escape when I see one, so I slip away from Shelby's soul-searching stare as soon as the speaker catches her attention.

I weave my way through the crowd of students. I'm itching to get down to the pranking, but I gotta find Moby and decide what we're going to throw at the Arch next.

I hear chunks of the announcement whenever I walk near a speaker.

"Assembly . . . blah, blah . . . elections . . . blah . . ."

I know exactly where to look for Moby. He's probably in his favorite stall in the upstairs boys' room, avoiding Shelby (and everyone else) until the second bell rings. I'm starting up the staircase with my head down, deep in thought, when I run into something very dense.

"You should watch where you're going," the Arch says, pushing me away.

I catch the railing and stop myself from tumbling backward down the stairs.

"Chubby-Jet-Ski?" he asks. He knows how to say

my name. He messes it up on purpose so nobody thinks he knows me. Plus, thanks to him I'm the only bald kid in sixth grade, so who else could it be?

"What do you want?"

"From you? Nothing. I'm just surprised I didn't find a dead fish or something in my locker this morning."

I roll my eyes but also mentally add *dead fish in locker* to my list of potential pranks.

"Vill vee see you at zee assembly?" he says.

Since he turned into the Arch, he feels the need to point out my accent. The way I sound makes most people assume I'm Russian. It takes a special kind of stupid to think I sound German.

The fact that he actually acknowledged my existence to tell me about the assembly is worrisome.

"Do I have a choice?"

He thinks for a minute. "I guess not."

I try to step around him, but he moves to block me.

"Get a good seat. You're gonna want to hear real good."

"*Well*," I correct. You would think people could at least learn to speak their first language properly.

He glances past me and does a chin raise to some kids coming up the stairs. Then he eyes me like he'd probably look at a dead fish in his locker. "Whatevs, Commie!" He pushes past and high-fives the kids on the landing. I think about explaining to him that Poland is a parliamentary republic, not a Communist country, but the second bell starts ringing. More sweat forms on my head as I take the stairs. I don't like the idea of a special assembly, and I really don't like the fact that the Arch is so excited about it. He knows I've made it my mission to ruin his undeserved reputation, and he is not about to let me get away with it.

If there's one thing I know to be true, it's this: There isn't much room to hide something up your sleeve in a cutoff muscle shirt.

CHAPTER 2

The assembly is after lunch, so I have all morning to worry why the Arch is so happy about it. Apparently, my usual tormentors are glad to be back from break too.

"Look out, here comes the Dalai Lame-a!" someone hollers as I make my way between homeroom and English class. People laugh—I take it as a compliment.

I'm in the cafeteria first, like always. Moby shows up after everyone has their food and is seated. He stands just inside the door, scanning the room for me, even though I always sit in the same spot—last table on the left, next to the trash cans. He's gone to school here just as long as the rest of us, but he always looks like a new kid on his first day.

Even though we've been inseparable since second grade, I'm not positive but I'm pretty sure that his stepmom picks out his clothes for him. What sixth grader chooses to wear corduroy and plaid? He's also the last kid on the planet that still uses a comb. The part in his hair is so perfect, it could be used to calibrate scientific instruments. I suspect this may be the Colonel's contribution. I can't hold it against him, though. If I had hair, I'd probably run home every day after school just to run a comb through it. *Enjoy it while it lasts*, *Mobe.*

He takes extra time in the cafeteria enjoying his homemade hummus and carrot platter. For once I don't rush him. We're in no hurry to join the pile of kids pushing through the doors of the gymnasium for the assembly.

Alanmoore was built in the early 1900s, and the gym hasn't been updated since. The basketball court was built below floor level, like a swimming pool, and the creaky wooden bleachers rise steeply into the rafters. The lighting is antique too, and combined with the sharp angle of the stands, it creates plenty of shadowy spaces at the top of the gym, the kind of spaces where you go when you don't want to be a part of the crowd. That's where we like to sit.

Mr. Mayer opens the assembly with the Pledge of Allegiance. He doesn't recite the pledge himself—he just scans the bleachers, making sure kids who aren't taking it seriously know he's watching them. When the pledge is done, Coach Farkas picks up the microphone and steps to the center of the gym. He waits a minute for nonexistent applause to die down before he speaks.

"Quick announcement before this school thing," he grunts, tugging up the waistband of his sweatpants. "As you know, the track team has been county champs for twenty-six straight years."

A sharp whoop rings out from the stands where the jocks are sitting. The Arch sits in the middle of the pack, nodding his approval.

"Go, Kangaroos," Coach says before continuing.

"We have an excellent squad, but that doesn't mean it can't get better."

The jocks murmur among themselves, probably wondering if they've just been insulted or not. I look at Moby and roll my eyes. The whole school knows what Coach Farkas is driving at. Track is the one sport the Arch doesn't do, and the coach wants him on the team like gravity wants a fat kid.

Sports are the source of what I call the popularity vortex. It's like the Bermuda Triangle—only instead of ships and planes getting lost, it's common sense that disappears. Kids get sucked into the vortex and go along with whatever the cool kids want.

"Tryouts are this week after school," Coach says. "If you think you have the stuff"—he turns and looks directly at the Arch—"you come see me. I'll make you a champion." He winks at the Arch, then hands the mic back to the principal.

Mr. Mayer is about to talk when Coach Farkas runs back and snatches the microphone again.

"Go, Roos!" he yells, and the student body explodes in applause.

We've won the county track title every year since Coach Farkas was on the team himself in sixth grade. It's something to be proud of, I guess. It's the one sport I don't have an official policy on because it's basically the only one that hasn't become the Arch Show yet.

Mr. Mayer wrestles the mic from Farkas. "Thanks, Coach Farkas. I'm willing to bet we've got another winner on our hands—or should I saaaay, feet!" The applause ends instantly. The lame joke floats in the silence like a turd in a punch bowl.

Moby gets the punch line a few seconds later and lets out a loud "HA!" that echoes around the old gymnasium. Everyone turns to look up into the rafters. I want to shrivel up and disappear, but no one can see us up here anyway.

"Anywhooo," Mr. Mayer goes on, "we're here to talk about something just as exciting as our track team—student government." Somehow the silence deepens. Someone in the lower section sneezes, and it sounds like a squeaky chew toy hit with a sledgehammer. Some kids laugh.

"This week you will all get to elect a treasurer, secretary, vice president, and most important, student body president."

More murmurs.

Instinctively I glance at the Arch. To my disappointment, he actually seems to be paying attention for once.

"This is a huge responsibility, since the student government is in charge of all social activities. Most important of all, they are your voice to the faculty in all matters, from student clubs to fund-raising to sports."

I'm starting to see why the Arch was giving me the hungry-coyote grin earlier.

"Anyone interested in running for student government should come see me for the paperwork and . . ." Movement in the crowd stops Mr. Mayer in midsentence. I don't have to look to know what the ruckus is about.

The Arch stands in the middle of the group of jocks. The only lightbulb in the old building that throws off a decent amount of light is directly over his head, shining down on him like a sunbeam through the clouds.

"Mr. Mayer, I'd like to volunteer!" The Arch's voice booms in a very student-body-presidential way.

Mr. Mayer stares at the Arch. "Um, it's not something you volunteer for exactly."

But his protest is too late. The Arch Show has already started. As though following an unspoken command, the crowd parts, and the Arch makes his way down the bleachers toward Mr. Mayer. He vaults the railing and drops the six feet to the floor of the gym. Mr. Mayer and the rest of the teachers watch dumbfounded as he struts across the court. He plucks the microphone out of Mr. Mayer's hand and turns toward the students.

"I, Archer Norris, officially volunteer to be your president!"

The students erupt in more applause and stomp the wooden bleachers so hard the building trembles.

I read Mr. Mayer's lips as he leans over to Coach Farkas. "It doesn't work that way," he says.

Coach Farkas doesn't respond; he just claps away like a trained seal.

I'm starting to see why the Arch was so happy in the stairwell. If he becomes the official voice of the students in all things, it will only be a matter of time before he makes it illegal to be me. If he becomes student body president, no one will ever take my word over his again. He'll for sure use his power to make life miserable for me.

Mr. Mayer wrestles the mic back. "It doesn't work that way, Archer. You have to have a platform and a debate, *and* you have to win the election."

Archer yanks the mic back and addresses the crowd. "I have a *platform*, and there's no *debate* about it. If I get made president, I promise to clean up this school." He waves a finger over the crowd of cheering students and then points it directly into the rafters where Moby and I are. The assembled students do a muted "*Ooooh!*"

My stomach flops. I'm not being paranoid; he wants to be president to mess with me.

Mr. Mayer leans over to Coach Farkas and mouths, "What does that even mean?"

I know what it means. It means he will figure out a way to use his power against me any way he can. I'm not sure if the student body president can get someone expelled, but if it can be done, Archer Norris will figure out how to do it.

When you combine my reputation as a troublemaker with his ability to get away with whatever he wants, I'm in deep doo-doo if he gets elected. I guess I couldn't expect my classmates to endure years of my pranks without some kind of payback eventually. Stink bombs, greased toilet seats, and drinking fountains rigged to squirt you in the crotch so it looks like you peed your pants are not precision tactics. Over the years there've been lots of civilian casualties. Once, Moby and I unscrewed the showerheads in the locker room and put fabric dye in them. It seemed like a foolproof plan at the time. I thought the Arch and his buddies were the only kids who actually showered at school. What I didn't know is that the girls' volleyball team uses the shower room after morning workouts. The fifth-grade Smurf attack was never officially pinned on me, but everyone sort of knew who did it. Even so, promising to put an end to my shenanigans isn't a good enough reason to elect him student body president. Is it?

"And," the Arch continues, "if I win the presidency, I promise"—he pauses for effect—"to join the Alanmoore track team and win another county title!"

The Arch raises his arms in a victory pose and drops the microphone like he just won a rap battle. It screeches when it hits the ground, but the roar of applause drowns the earsplitting sound.

Our archnemesis relationship was built on lack of respect and mutual dislike. But if he is going to be president of the school, this thing is about to go to a whole new level. He'll instantly be in Mr. Mayer's inner circle. Every little thing that breaks in this crumbly old school he'll blame on me. Who's the principal going to believe when it comes down to it: me or Mr. Perfect?

Moby and I need a plot to take the Arch down a peg or two, and we need one fast. We have to make him unpopular enough that someone else will have a shot at winning the election.

"It doesn't work that way," Mr. Mayer continues to protest, but nobody can hear him over the roar of the crowd.

Maybe it does now, I think.

CHAPTER 3

I feel sorry for Moby having to trim his grandpa's toenails, but the Colonel is a gold mine of good prank ideas, and he comes up with his best stuff while Moby works on his feet. The Colonel says it's called "taking one for the team." Whatever you call it, I need some fresh ideas, and the Colonel is my best bet.

He likes to start his monthly toenail trimming at exactly 2000 hours (eight o'clock). My mom drops me off with time to spare. I knock on the Dicks' door at 1945.

They live only a few blocks away, but in the city a lot can change in a few blocks. Moby's house looks like a miniature version of the White House. Our house looks like the shed where the people who own Moby's house keep their lawn mower.

Moby answers the door with a queasy look.

"You didn't start yet, did you?" I ask.

He shakes his head and lets me in.

Moby's dad and stepmom are in the kitchen cleaning up the dishes from dinner. They are cool parents, I guess. They pretty much leave Moby alone. They're both lawyers, but you'd never know it by the way they dress at home. Here they look like college students getting ready to protest something. They get their lawyer clothes dry-cleaned at our shop, and my parents never get tired of talking about how nicely the Dicks dress. If they only knew. They don't hang out together, thank goodness.

I walk into the kitchen, and Moby's stepmom puts down a wineglass and gives me a hug. She's wearing a sweater that looks like a failed attempt to repair a badly damaged fishing net. If she hugged me any harder, the garment would rub some skin off my face.

"Maciek!" she says, giving me a fake kiss on each

cheek. She's one of the few people who use my real name. The kiss thing is weird, but at least she says my name right. "Have you gotten taller?"

I look down at my feet; they don't look any farther away than usual.

"No."

"Well, then I must be shrinking." She laughs a little too hard.

When Mrs. Dick lets me go, Moby's dad shoves his enormous hand at me. "Wassup, Jet Ski!" He could crush a lump of coal into a diamond with his grip, and he likes to prove it to me every time I visit. "You missed out. We just had some awesome eggplant and quinoa casserole. There's probably some left if you're hungry."

"Sounds delicious, but I'm allergic to eggs," I say, dodging the vegan bullet. Behind him, Mrs. Dick sneakily unscrews the lid of a jar of cookie butter and takes a gigantic swipe with her finger. She offers the jar to Moby, who does the same, then she quietly replaces the lid and stashes the jar in the pantry while Mr. Dick is distracted pumping my arm.

When I get my hand back, I make sure nothing's broken and shake the blood back into it.

His smile looks like he wants to sell me toothpaste. "So, what are you two up to tonight? No good?"

"What makes you say that, sir?" I ask.

"Save the 'sir' for my dad." He pokes his thumb toward the stairs. "I told you before, call me Jason, Chub."

We stand there in awkward silence for a moment. He has been telling me that for years, but it feels like a trick. I can't imagine my dad telling one of my friends to call him Kasmir. Moby kicks my foot.

"Okay—Jason," I say.

He laughs like I just told him he won the lottery and slaps me on the shoulder. "Right on, man."

"I better . . ." Moby nods toward the stairs.

"Oh, yeah, yeah, don't keep the commandant waiting." Jason flips a mock salute.

"Levi?" he calls when we are almost to the stairs. We stop and turn around. "What are our two favorite words?"

"Antioxidants," Moby recites.

Jason makes his finger into a pistol, points it at us, and winks.

"I'll take 'em before bed."

We turn and head up the stairs. I whisper to Moby, "'Antioxidant' is only one word."

"Just keep walking," he whispers back.

The Colonel throws each of us a quick salute when we enter the theater room. He's in the same chair as always, front row center.

"Perfect timing. Show starts in a few minutes," he says in his snarly army voice.

"What are we watching tonight, sir?" I ask.

The Colonel sneers. "It's a show about a bunch of terrorists trying to destroy our way of life!"

"Is it a spy show?"

"*Whale Wars*." Moby rolls his eyes.

The Colonel makes a sound like air leaking out of a tire. The show hasn't even started yet and he's already grumpy. This is going to be good.

Whale Wars is a reality show where environmental activists try to save whales from getting harpooned by Japanese whalers. I guess people watch it because they have too much time on their hands; either that or they really care about whales. The Colonel watches it like it's a sport, and he roots hard for the Japanese. Every time the whalers launch a harpoon, he raises his arms in a V, and every time the protestors ram the whalers' ship, he boos at the screen. I don't think he realizes that they're trying to show the whalers as the bad guys. Maybe it's just a matter of how you look at it. Moby's parents watch the show in another room, rooting for the other team.

While I catch the Colonel up on what I did over the break, Moby gets down on the floor at his grandpa's feet and lays down a towel embroidered with the insignia of the US Army. Then he unzips a black case, revealing the Colonel's pedicure kit. It's like something an evil dentist would use to torture answers out of someone. It's actually kind of cool, but I make sure I don't express any interest. I absolutely do not want to get a lesson in how the tools work—that way I can never get drafted for TD. Colonel Dick calls that "plausible deniability."

Moby is about to start trimming when the Colonel

stops him. "Wait! Have you been vaccinated against fun today?"

Moby shakes his head. "I take my vitamins before bed, Grandpa."

The Colonel chuckles at his joke, then points at his feet. "As you were," he says. And Moby starts chunking away. Right before the show starts, the Colonel says, "Just be glad I taught you how to swallow those tablets so you don't have to get suppositories anymore."

Moby shudders.

"What are suppositories?" I ask.

The Colonel chuckles.

"I don't want to talk about it," Moby says. He snaps off a huge shard of yellow toenail, which hits the wall on the far side of the room.

Moby doesn't get to see most of the show. He's too busy dodging chunks of toenail that the clippers send flying around the room like shrapnel.

"Hey!" the Colonel yells when Moby clips a little too close. "Go easy with those trimmers, Private."

"I'm not in the army, Grandpa."

"And with that attitude, you never will be."

If TD is any indication of army life, I'm pretty sure Moby is fine just being a civilian.

When the show is over and the Colonel has his slippers on, I see my chance. If there's one thing that gets the Colonel fired up, it's people with long hair protesting stuff. If I can channel the Colonel's annoyance with the "dirty hippies" on the show trying to stop the whalers, I can probably get something good out of him.

"Boy, those hippies sure are undisciplined," I say. Discipline is the Colonel's favorite subject.

He cocks an eyebrow at me, and so does Moby.

I shake my head to show him I share his frustration. "I wonder how someone could teach them a lesson."

Moby looks at me like I'm nuts. But then the Colonel runs a hand over his boot-brush haircut and starts telling stories about basic training. Moby nods at me knowingly. He sees where I'm going with this.

"Back in boot camp we had a guy who would never come out of the bathroom in time. The whole platoon had to do extra push-ups as punishment."

"No discipline," I say.

"Exactly." He shoots me a look but keeps going. "Let me tell you what we did to help him speed things up. . . ."

Without realizing it, he lays out a plan for a plot to embarrass the Arch in front of the whole school. If this works like he says it does, the Arch won't be able to show his face at school again, let alone have enough *cool* left over to win the election. Like I said, the Colonel's a gold mine.

Before I leave, we sneak into the Colonel's room and use his phone to make a call. The phone has a round dial instead of buttons, but we figure it out.

Luckily, Darby, Delvin, and Darwin McQueen are still awake. I'm not sure which one of the triplets I talk to, but he agrees they will meet me after school tomorrow.

If you slide between the trash Dumpster and the recycling Dumpster behind the school, you'll find a small alcove, like a brick cave built into the side of the building. The smell from the Dumpsters keeps kids from getting curious and discovering it. I found it while I was looking for a place to hide from a group of basketball players who wanted to touch my head for luck before a game. I think it's where they used to deliver coal to heat the school in the old days. Now it's where I go when I need a little privacy to conduct business.

All three McQueens meet me there after the final bell.

The triplets have a tattered leather hat they all share. It's a flat, floppy cap like you'd see on a kid selling newspapers in a really old movie. You can talk to any of them, but only the one wearing the hat will respond. That's the way they like to play it. It's cost them a few detentions here and there, but I think the teachers have learned to respect the system. Either that or they've just gotten tired of fighting it.

I'm pretty sure Darwin is the one in the hat today.

"G'day, Chub."

"Guys," I say.

The other two nod but don't speak.

"Make it quick, boyo. You're cutting into video game time."

"Like I said last night, I need a level-three plug

job." The triplets specialize in wet work: sabotage of water fixtures and plugging of toilets. They trade grins among themselves. This job is right up their alley.

The hatted one nods. "Did you bring the payment?"

The McQueens live by the Joker's advice: "If you're good at something, never do it for free." And they are the best at what they do. I hold up three tardy slips, with their names, that I "borrowed" from Mr. Mayer's office earlier in the day. The McQueens aren't political like me and Moby. They are in it for the pay, not the principle. Also, I suspect, because they just like causing havoc. I guess I trust them because their parents are from Ireland and their bright-orange hair makes them magnets for kids looking for someone to pick on.

I hesitate before handing the slips over. "Do you have the goods?"

The spokesman nods to the other two. They reach into their messenger bags and pull out the tools of their trade. The one on the left (Darby, I think) proudly holds up a roll of superabsorbent paper towels in one hand and a thick Sunday newspaper in the other. The one on the right (Delvin?) brandishes two family-size cans of extra-chunky beef stew.

As a rule, I try not to smile in front of anyone but Moby, but I really have to fight to keep the grin off my face as I imagine the mess the triplets are about to make. I nod and hand over the slips. The hat-bearer looks them over, then passes them to the one with the newspaper, who tucks them into his pocket with a wink.

Darwin (?) tips the brim of his hat to me. "Pleasure as always, Chub."

They spin on their heels and head off to fulfill their end of the bargain.

Ten minutes later Moby meets me in the back corner of the locker room. He hands me the bottle of dish soap I requested in a brown paper bag. His face is bright red, like it gets when he's nervous. I recognize the look. It's his look of panic when we are about to break the rules. He breathes in giant, whooping gulps. I need to calm him down before he loses it and chickens out.

I put the soap in the pocket of my sweatshirt and

give him the paper bag. "Breathe into this."

He inflates and deflates the bag violently a few times before his breathing slows to a normal rate, then he wipes sweat from his forehead and nods to me that he's ready. I run through the plan with him one more time. All that's left is to wait for the McQueens to do their thing, and Moby can get to work.

Less than a minute passes before the voice of the school secretary, Mrs. Osborne, crackles over the intercom.

"Mr. Kraley, please go to the upstairs boys' room immediately!" Her voice quivers like a dog pooping out a peach pit. "There's been a . . . an . . . accident!" She must forget to take her finger off the button, because before the speaker crackles off: "Dear Lord, is that a mushroom?"

Moby and I chuckle. Once again the McQueens have proven they are worth whatever price they ask.

We quickly take up our position behind the door to the coach's private office. Right on cue the door flies open, almost smashing us, but I catch it just in time. Mr. Kraley bursts into the hall, buttoning up his custodian uniform. As he runs the other way, Moby and I spring from our hiding spot and slip into the empty office.

The mascot costume of the Alanmoore Kangaroos lies in a heap on the floor where Mr. Kraley jumped out of it when he heard the announcement.

The kangaroo mascot costume doesn't fit any of the kids in school, so Mr. Kraley gets paid to wear it at games and special occasions, like track tryouts. I feel a little bad for putting him through what he's about to discover in the boys' room, but for the plan to work I need him out of the suit.

Moby winces when he gets a whiff of the inside of the costume. I've never once seen it in my parents' shop to be cleaned, and the inside has absorbed years' worth of Mr. Kraley's BO. Moby makes a face similar to the one I imagine Mr. Kraley will make when he sees the result of the McQueens' plug job.

He holds the suit as far from his nose as possible. "It smells like the time the Colonel's ingrown toenail got infected!"

I sympathize with the kid, I really do, but we are

too far into the plan to stop now. To show solidarity, I grab the giant foam kangaroo head and take a whiff. It takes an act of sheer will not to throw up. "It's not that bad."

Moby rolls his eyes and snatches the head back from me. "Next time I'm coming up with the plan and you're wearing someone's dirty laundry."

That will never happen. I am the brains here.

"We can talk about that," I say. I turn to check the hall through the small window in the door, and when I turn back, Moby is stripped to his underwear and stepping into the suit.

I slap my forehead. "Why are you naked?"

"I don't want my clothes to stink. Duh."

Like I said, I'm the brains.

I help him pull the suit on and zip it up, then hand him the head. He takes one last deep breath of fresh locker room air and then pulls it on, completing the costume.

"How do I look?" he asks through the mesh-covered hole in the kangaroo's neck.

I look him over. The suit is four sizes too big,

and it slumps on his scrawny frame. He resembles an experiment to cross a giant rat with a shar-pei.

"Perfect," I say, doing the snaps that keep the head from falling off. "Oops, almost forgot." I tuck the bottle of dish soap into the kangaroo pouch.

He gives me the thumbs-up sign.

"Remember, in and out quick, like we planned."

"Uh-huh."

"And?"

"And absolutely no improvising," he recites.

The library is on the fourth floor and looks over the football field and track, where the tryouts are held. I sneak in and creep behind the stacks of books farthest from the librarian's office. I don't have to be that stealthy; she's older than the school, and even if she's awake, she probably couldn't hear a herd of buffalo stampede through the nonfiction section. I make it to my lookout window just as Moby hops out of the locker room toward the track, and I watch through my dad's borrowed binoculars as he clumsily makes his way toward the tryouts.

So far, so good.

As usual, the Arch is the center of attention. He's easy to spot, even from a distance, since he's half a foot taller than pretty much everyone else trying out. The only other kid his size is Julius Jackson, the star of the track team.

The two of them are racing side by side, but at the end the Arch pulls way out in front and leaves Julius in his dust. The Arch waves to the few kids who've gathered in the bleachers, then jogs off to the next event. Julius lies on the track by the finish line, gasping for breath and shaking his head. The group of kids who normally high-five him when he wins a race is gone. They've forgotten all about him. Now they're orbiting the new fastest kid on the track team.

The Arch is making a big show of flopping over the high jump bar, and Coach Farkas scribbles notes on his clipboard and giggles like a little girl with a new pony. At least the coach will be preoccupied when Moby pours the dish soap into the Gatorade.

Even among jocks, kids sort themselves into ranks by popularity. That means the Arch and his buddies get to drink first. If this works the way the Colonel claimed, the Arch—and maybe a few other unfortunate victims, including Coach Farkas—will be lucky to make it halfway to the gym before pooping his pants. And it's pretty tough to look presidential with a tracksuit full of explosive butt-chowder.

The mascot is at every school function, so nobody pays particular attention to the mutant kangaroo skulking toward the Gatorade. Moby waits for the crowd to be distracted before lifting the lid off of the giant tank of purple liquid. Then he pulls out the bottle of soap and squeezes it into the tank with both hands.

"Now get out of there!" I say under my breath.

Moby puts the empty bottle into his pouch, screws the lid back on the tank, and starts to walk away. I almost let out the breath I'm holding—almost.

He's ten feet away and no one has so much as glanced at him when he stops in his tracks, turns, and walks back to the Gatorade.

"What are you doing?" I whisper to myself, then glance around to make sure Mrs. Belfry didn't hear. Moby looks ultrasuspicious as he creeps back to the table like a villain in a cartoon. Panic washes over me as he grabs the lid and spins it back off the tank! He's improvising and there's nothing I can do to stop him. I almost can't watch what happens next.

He reaches a paw into the jug and stirs the Gatorade.

I put down the binoculars and slap my forehead in disbelief. When he's done, he pulls his paw out and shakes it off. The gray fur is stained purple all the way up to the elbow.

He's halfway across the track on his way back to school when I spot a commotion out of the corner of my eye. The Arch has finished his high jump exhibition, and now he's launching shot puts around the field like artillery fire. A crowd gathers to watch him—put?—but something is different about his posture. For once the Arch is more interested in someone else's actions than his own. His gaze is fixed on the deflated kangaroo shuffling across the track toward the locker room.

He tilts his head like a curious dog as he watches the purple-armed creature. Then the look on his face changes. He may not have figured it all out, but apparently he's figured out enough to try to stop it.

My blood runs cold. Moby is as good as caught.

The Arch looks over the heads of the crowd toward the only thing that could've stained the costume—the Gatorade. Coach Farkas is holding the cooler above his head, about to grab the spout to pour the soapy purple beverage into his mouth. The Arch is too far away to save him.

The next three seconds unfold in slow motion. I turn the binoculars back to the Arch; he's lifting a shot put into the crook of his neck. He turns away from the normal landing zone, crouches low, and explodes back up, launching the heavy metal ball over the heads of the crowd. I stare in disbelief as it flies through the air in the completely wrong direction. Has the Arch lost his mind?

The question is answered a second later when the shot put smashes into the Gatorade cooler and knocks it out of Coach Farkas's hands. The force of the impact crushes the cooler and sprays Gatorade everywhere, coating Farkas from head to toe. First he looks stunned, then angry as he glares around for the culprit. I've fogged up the lenses of the binoculars, but

I wipe them on my sweatshirt in time to see the Arch jog up to him and say something that seems to calm him down. Coach Farkas flicks a handful of purple bubbles off his shoulder.

Moby! He's been spotted by the Arch, and even with a head start there's no way he can outrun him in the costume.

I scan the track with the binoculars. Halfway up the path to the gym lies a kangaroo head. A few yards farther up, in a wrinkled heap, is the hide of a purple-pawed mascot. Moby is nowhere to be seen. At least he left his underwear on.

I glance back to see if anyone is going after him. What I see makes my blood a few degrees colder. The Arch is looking directly back at me, a sharky grin plastered on his face.

CHAPTER 4

The next day at school I wait for the hammer of justice to drop. The Arch knows it was me, and he's way too much of a butt-kisser to let me get away with something like this. I may have finally pushed my luck too far.

What makes my stomach turn is the fact that I haven't seen Moby since he pulled his Houdini act. The kid can disappear like a fart in a hurricane when the heat is on, but he always answers my call later. I haven't heard a word from him since things went wrong, and he didn't meet me before school, either. Moby might improvise at the wrong time, but he doesn't improvise when it comes to his schedule. Everything in his life has to happen at its proper time or he gets . . . weird. He missed his afternoon toilet break once and convinced his dad he needed two days off school to get back in sync. I'm starting to think that maybe he moved to Brazil to avoid Mr. Mayer. Maybe he thinks I'm mad about him ruining the plot. Don't get me wrong—I was, but now I just want to make sure he's all right.

The desk next to me squeaks. I turn, expecting to see Moby, but it's not him. Other than the Arch, it's the last person I want to talk to. Shelby peers at me, her bird-girl stare magnified by her glasses. She purses her lips in an obnoxious smirk. I didn't think it was possible for her to be more annoying than she already was, but I was wrong.

She folds her hands on the desk, clearly wanting me to ask what the smirk is about. I've never started a conversation with a girl before, and I don't intend my first one to be with a girl as annoying as Shelby.

"Did you hear about track tryouts?" she whispers.

I don't want to look interested, but I'm dying to

hear what everyone is saying. I shrug, knowing she'll tell me no matter what.

"Someone put soap in the Gatorade."

I bite my lip to keep from grinning.

"But Archer Norris foiled the scheme just before Coach Farkas took a fateful sip," she says, sounding all dreamy.

She pulls a cloth handkerchief out of the cuff of her sweater and dabs her forehead. My urge to smile vanishes. She thinks the Arch was the good guy yesterday! And did she really need to use the words "foiled" and "fateful" in the same sentence?

"Good for Archer." I hope it's the end of the conversation. The first bell rings and kids fill the classroom.

"Still," she whispers, "it almost worked."

What is that supposed to mean? Does she know it was me? If so, what would it cost to keep her quiet? Maybe I can swipe her a couple of old-lady sweaters out of the funeral home's donation pile at the dry cleaning shop.

It doesn't matter. I know the Arch's heroics are all that kids will talk about. I clench my hands in frustration. I'm sick of being foiled, but at least Moby didn't get caught and expelled for streaking.

Moby slinks into the classroom right as the second bell rings. He's wearing his dad's law school sweatshirt, which fits him about as well as a parachute. He sits at his desk, his hands jammed in the pouch pocket of the sweatshirt. When he finally glances my way, I shrug at him in the universal sign for *What gives?*

He pulls his hand partway out of the pocket and shoves up his sleeve. My scalp flushes instantly. His arm is stained purple all the way to his elbow.

A quick scan of the room tells me no else has caught him purple-handed. He jams his hand back into the pocket, and I slap my head hard enough that some kids turn around to look.

"You know, Maciek," Shelby says, sitting extra upright, "the drama club meets on Mondays and Wednesdays. You should come check it out."

"Hurm," I mumble. I have about as much interest in the drama club as I have in helping my mom shop for bras, but it might come in handy someday for a plot. I make a mental note to show up at least once.

Mr. Funk comes into the room, late as usual, just as the voice of Mr. Mayer crackles over the intercom. "Good mooooorning, Alanmoore. A few announcements to start the day. Track tryouts went well despite some . . . shenanigans."

At least we get *some* recognition. Shelby shoots me a sideways glance, which I ignore.

"The list of students who made the team will be posted blah, blah, blah . . ." As Mr. Mayer babbles on, Mrs. Osborne scurries into the room without her usual knock and hands Mr. Funk a small slip of paper. She races out again without her usual embarrassed smile.

Mr. Funk glances at the piece of paper, then at me. This is it. Here comes the hammer. Mr. Funk doesn't have to say anything—the look on his face says it all. I put my books back into my bag and stand as kids turn to see who is in trouble. Shelby gives me a worried look.

This isn't the first time I've been busted. The important part is for me to look calm and cool as I make the long walk out of the silent classroom. There's no point in causing havoc if you're going to look all apologetic as soon as you get caught. It's just the cost of doing business. Mrs. Osborne won't look me in the eye as I walk into the school office. She may as well wear a flashing sign that says DISAPPOINTED.

I grab the seat by the door to the principal's office and wait to be summoned, but my butt cheeks barely kiss pine before the door opens.

". . . appreciate your help. It will be dealt with."

I look up and there in front of me is the Arch. He gives me a nasty smile, then turns back toward the office.

"And congratulations," Mr. Mayer practically gushes. "I hear you are our new track team captain."

The Arch shrugs. "I guess so." The fake humility in his voice makes me want to barf. "It's the least I can do for this school." He looks down at me and winks. I put my finger in my mouth like I'm trying to gag.

"From what Coach Farkas says, the throw that saved him from drinking the tainted Gatorade was a new county record."

The Arch puts on his most casual look. "By, like, eight feet, or whatever."

I almost sprain a muscle rolling my eyes. Here

I am trying to lead sixth graders out of the middle school popularity vortex, and this meathead is getting patted on the back for chucking a metal ball?

I make an exaggerated coughing noise that sounds a lot like a word you can get detention for using.

The Arch pretends to notice me. "I think your next *appointment* is here, Mr. Mayer." He swings his backpack onto his shoulder, nearly smashing me in the nose with it.

"Good luck, cube ball," he says under his breath so Mrs. Osborne can't hear.

"I think you mean 'cue ball.' 'Cube ball' is an oxymoron."

"What did you just call me?" He fake-lurches at me.

I flinch and it makes him grin. "Have a nice day, Mrs. Osborne," he says in the voice kids use only when they're sucking up to adults.

Mr. Mayer's voice has authority in it I've never heard before. "Mr. Trzebiatowski! Please step into my office."

My pranks have landed me in the principal's office before, so it doesn't have the mystique it had when I was younger. Still, I don't want to be here any longer than I have to be. I shut the door behind me and take my regular seat.

Mr. Mayer sits behind his desk, looking at me over his glasses.

"Well, what do you have to say for yourself this time?"

I consider my options. I could deny it, but he knows it was me.

I could say it was all a big misunderstanding, but he knows it wasn't.

I could plead insanity; everyone knows the story about a kid a few years back that everyone called the Fink. The Fink was a legendary troublemaker at Alanmoore who once got away with pantsing the old principal at a pep rally. They say he claimed temporary insanity caused by inhaling chalk dust while cleaning erasers. But it's probably just a rumor. For all I know, the guy might've never existed.

In the end I decide none of those responses are my style.

"Mr. Mayer," I say, looking him straight in the eye, "it was me. I admit to the whole thing."

He lets out a long breath, takes off his glasses, and rubs his eyes. Then he stares right back at me without blinking. Finally he lets out another long breath and put his glasses back on. He slumps in his chair and loosens his tie.

"I know it was you, Maciek," he says. "And I can't keep covering for you."

I walked in once while Mr. Mayer was playing poker on his school laptop. Ever since then he's gone pretty easy on me. The rumor is that the old principal was fired when the school board found out he was deejaying on the weekends. I guess Mr. Mayer doesn't want me mentioning his hobby to anyone. I don't understand why anyone would want to play a game where losing actually costs you money, but whatever.

When I get busted for anything minor, he doesn't mention it to my parents. In exchange I keep the online poker to myself. He keeps his job, and I get the little bit of space I need to mess with the Arch. It works very well for both of us.

I stand up to walk out of the office and head back to my classroom. I figure since nobody actually drank the

Gatorade, it'll be easy for him to let this one slide. I'm at the door when he says, "Archer Norris knows it was you. It has to look like I'm dealing with the situation."

I freeze, the doorknob in my hand. He has a point. If I get away with every plot I pull, it will start to look suspicious. I'll need to do a little time to keep my get-out-of-jail-free card open.

"This Saturday, then?" he says.

I let go of the knob and turn around. "I can't do Saturday."

My parents are afraid that being raised in America instead of in Poland, like they were, is making me soft, so they make me work at their dry cleaning shop on Saturdays to "build my character." Apparently, they think the main ingredients in a kid's character are sweat and lack of sunlight.

I'm supposed to go to the theater and hang out with Jarek after school this afternoon, then watch the movie with Moby after Jarek's done splicing it together. I *could* stay after today and still make it to the movie, and my parents would never have to ask where I was. "I can do detention today."

"This really seems like a Saturday offense."

"Detention today and you let some of the students overhear you saying it was me and how difficult I was to catch?"

"You tried to poison the track team. You're lucky you aren't getting suspended!"

If he insists on Saturday, the grief I'll catch from my dad will make detention look like a vacation. My parents work fourteen hours a day so we can afford to live in a neighborhood with a decent school. They won't be very understanding if I get kicked out.

"How about detention today, and I'll see if my dad will clean the kangaroo suit for free?"

He sighs.

"That thing is a mess. It's probably the first time it's touched soap in a long time."

He lowers his eyebrows, so I know he doesn't like it. "Today will work fine."

I smile. "See you in detention."

He doesn't smile back, which concerns me. If I ever push him too far and he calls my bluff, I'll get the ten-million-pound poo hammer from my parents no matter what. Taking him down with me will be small consolation at that point.

I'm about to leave when he picks up a yellow sheet of paper off his desk and holds it out to me. "You know, there are other ways to make a difference."

I take the paper from him. It's a registration form for the school elections. I look it over for a second, fold it, and stuff it into my pocket.

"Turn it in by tomorrow if you want to run," he says as I walk out of the office.

How can Mr. Mayer spend all day, every day, in a school full of kids and not understand how things work? According to the laws of middle school popularity, the Arch is pretty much destined to become student body president.

Unless I figure out a way to show the school that he's not as cool as they think he is.

CHAPTER 5

I heard this saying once. "It's not *what* you know, it's *who* you know." Well, I think what's actually important is *what* you know *about* who you know.

Because of the dirt I have on Mr. Mayer, I serve my detentions in solitary confinement. I don't have to sit in the room with all the kids who got caught texting or cheating on tests while the gym teacher forces them to study. I do my time in the library all by myself, where I can pass the hour looking through the stash of comic books I've hidden behind the emergency fire hose. I'm not going to say I look forward to it, exactly, but I do like being alone sometimes.

If I weren't in detention, Moby and I would be on our way to the Clairemont right now. But I am, and Moby shuffles around outside the window like a lost puppy while I'm locked up. He keeps looking up at the window like he wishes he were in here with me. But I was the mastermind of the plot. I'll serve the time for getting caught.

Mrs. Belfry, our librarian, supervises me during detention. I'm not sure exactly how old she is, but it's gotta be triple digits. Her hair has a purple tint that isn't found in nature, and I don't think she dyes it that way out of school spirit. I assume she's old enough to remember what life was like before electricity, because every time she flips on a light switch, she says, "Ooh," like she still can't believe it works.

The first time Mr. Mayer escorted me to the library for detention, Mrs. Belfry looked at us like a pair of unicorns had appeared through a portal and started piddling on the rug. Mr. Mayer sent me off to the other side of the library while he explained why I was here instead of with the general population. I couldn't hear everything he said, but a few words carried across the stacks of books: "immigrant," which seemed like a weird thing to say, and "gifted," which didn't bother me quite as much.

I always make sure to let Mrs. Belfry hear me mumbling to myself in the few Polish words I know as I thumb through books. It can't hurt if she thinks I'm "gifted" in two languages.

Whatever he actually said to her, I suppose I should be grateful. It bought me just enough cred to get into her good graces despite earning detention on a pretty regular basis.

"Mr. Trom-boz-ow-ski?" she says. I walk to her office door and stick my head inside. A flowery blast of old-lady perfume punches me square in the nose. "What have you gotten into today?"

I always have a story prepared. "Some boys from the track team were making Polish jokes."

She puts both hands over her heart and makes a small gasp.

"It just made me think of my uncle Stosh, so I told them to shut up, and one of them shoved me. I was going to shove him back when Mr. Mayer came around the corner, and here I am."

"That's awful!" She wrings her hands. "I went to school with lots of very nice Polish children. There's simply no call for that!"

I nod thoughtfully. "That's exactly what I told them. No call for that."

For a second I'm afraid she's going to get up and give me a hug, but at her age you probably get out of chairs only if the house is on fire.

I'm about to find a spot to read my comics when she points to a sleek new laptop on her desk. "Do you know anything about these?"

The sight of the laptop makes my head swim. We don't have a computer at home, since my dad doesn't want the government knowing what kind of Kleenex we buy or something. If I ever want to use one, I have to go to the public library or use Jarek's during the rare times he's not on it. If I play this right, it could be my chance to access the secrets of life, the universe, and everything, or at least look up news on some summer movies I can't wait to see. All I have to do is get by a two-hundred-year-old librarian.

"The school gave me this, and I . . ." She punches a couple of random keys and then throws up her hands. "The district has been trying to get me to retire for twenty years. If I can't figure out how to use this contraption, I won't be able to do my job anymore."

I try not to sound too eager. "I . . . could take a look."

A smile of relief spreads across her face. She stands up and offers me the chair. "Make sure you explain what you're doing so I can make it work later."

I sit at her desk and punch some keys to see what it can do.

She cranes her neck over my shoulder toward the screen. Her glasses are as thick as the polar ice caps. "I can't see from here. What's happening now?"

"I'm, uh, checking your *infarcation decryptor.* It looks like it's pretty old for such a new computer."

While Mrs. Belfry frets over her outdated IF decryptor, I type the most important question I can think of into the search bar.

Now that I have the key to all knowledge in the history of human existence, there's one question I need answered: "League of Honor finale release date?"

In less than a second I've got it. The greatest day of my life so far is going to be June 20, one week after school lets out for the summer.

"Yes!"

She wrings her hands. "Is it okay after all?"

For a second I forgot she was there. "Oh, yeah, it's good. But we need to reboot your *flux capacitor*."

"Will that take long?"

"Couple minutes," I say.

Mr. Mayer usually checks in every fifteen minutes or so to make sure I'm not having any fun. If I intend to have some, I need to do it quickly.

"This is all beyond me." She flicks her wrist at the laptop. "I'm going to go make some tea while you finish fixing the—*humph*."

I feel a little bad about tricking a nice old lady, but the feeling is outweighed by the sheer glee of having unsupervised access to a computer. I close the browser and scan the home screen.

An icon in the upper left-hand corner jumps out at me.

Administration.

Could it really be this simple? If this is what I think it is, and Mrs. Belfry is the only gatekeeper, I may jump right past infamous and move directly to legendary.

With a trembling finger I double-click the mouse. A box appears asking for my user ID and password.

I fumble around the desk for something with her full name on it. Finally I spot a plaque on the wall.

LIBRARIAN OF THE YEAR, 1958: IRMA BELFRY.

I type "IrmaBelfry" into the user ID line and then try to guess what her password might be. I type all the prehistoric librarian things I can think of: "books," "bingo," "soup." None of them work. What else could she possibly be into? I scan her office for a clue.

I don't have to look long. On the front of her desk is a gold frame with a picture of the fattest cat I've ever seen. He's wearing a little cat tuxedo complete with a top hat, and a cane is taped awkwardly to his paw. I'm pretty sure this is some sort of animal abuse.

"Mrs. Belfry?"

A moment later she appears in the doorway.

"Is everything all right?"

"I think so. You might want to stay back a few feet in case there's a flatumonium leak, though."

She backs up to a safe distance and wrings her hands some more.

I point at the picture. "I was just wondering, what's your cat's name?"

Her face lights up. "Oooh, isn't Mr. Darcy handsome?"

I fight back a smirk and type "MrDarcy" into the password box and click enter.

"He certain—" The screen goes blank for a second, then comes back up. What I see makes my eyes bulge.

Mrs. Belfry retreats slightly behind the door. "Why don't you call me when you're done." She scurries off.

All I can do is nod dumbly as I read the screen. What I have in front of me is the equivalent of winning the lottery. I'm looking at the faculty administration page, the control center for every grade, report, and record of every student in the school.

I'm in.

I find the search box and type in a name, and a few seconds later I'm looking at the permanent records of one of Alanmoore's students. I rub my hands together and giggle at my good fortune.

"Hello, Mr. Norris." I scroll down the page, scanning every grade he's ever gotten at Alanmoore. "Let's see what you've been up to since fifth grade."

For the last fifteen minutes of detention I tutor Mrs. Belfry on computer basics. She's almost mastered pressing the on button when my one-hour sentence is over. I'd probably have more luck teaching a turtle to defuse a nuclear bomb, but I feel guilty for abusing her trust, so it's the least I can do. Besides, if she gets fired, I'm out a computer.

When I finally breathe the sweet air of freedom again at three thirty, I can't wait to tell Moby the news about the computer. He isn't outside the window anymore, so I check all the bathrooms and the spot behind the Dumpsters. It isn't one of his usual bathroom times—the next one isn't until three forty-five—but sometimes he will vanish into thin air if he gets nervous. There were probably some kids around he wanted to avoid.

He always shows up in time for the movie, so I walk the three blocks over to the Clairemont alone. My parents are pretty protective, but they let me walk a few blocks on my own as long as I'm going to Moby's, the shop, or the Clairemont.

Jarek lets me in the back door. I try not to think about the place being haunted as he leads me across the old stage behind the movie screens, and down the maintenance corridor to the front of the building.

"Moby got here a few minutes ago," he says.

"He did? What's he doing?"

Jarek looks at me like it's the dumbest question ever.

"Oh, right. I'll wait for him in the theater."

"Ya, I'll bring him up. You are late; you up to something today?"

"There've been some developments we need to deal with," I admit.

We stop in the lobby. My cousin appears to ponder this. "I hear Archer Norris is new track team captain. Is this why?"

"How do you even know about that?"

"Moby told me."

I grumble.

"Why you mess with that kid? What he ever do to you?" Jarek asks.

My hand instinctively goes to my head, and I stuff it back into my pocket. "Sometimes you have to do what you have to do," I say.

He thinks about this for a second. "Well, just remember, the same goes for parents, too."

"What's that supposed to mean?" I ask, even though I think I already know.

"I know Uncle Kasmir. If he thinks you are misbehaving, he'll do what he has to do to stop it."

He's right. My dad won't hesitate to send me to Poland for a summer of hard labor on my uncle's potato farm if I give him a reason to. But some things are important enough to take the risk. "I'll keep that in mind," I say.

"*Dobry*," he says, which means "good" in Polish. "I send your friend up when he gets done."

I thank him and cut across the lobby toward the winding staircase that leads to the small theater where we have our sneak previews. Legend has it a gangster and his girlfriend died in a shoot-out in the stairwell back in the 1920s. Supposedly, if you touch the spot on the wall where the bullet holes used to be, the ghosts will appear to you during your movie. I never get close enough to use the handrail, let alone accidentally brush the wall. The building itself is creepy enough without having to worry about ghosts.

There are only twenty seats in the upstairs theater, and I take the one in the very center, where the sound is the best. I unpack the bag of snacks my mom prepared for me and Moby and arrange them on the seat next to me in order of sweetness, so that we can eat them in the proper sequence without having to look away from the screen. I'm folding up the paper bag when the curtain at the back of the theater parts and Jarek appears.

"Your friend is here," he says, and then winks.

What was that all about? A moment later it

becomes clear as Shelby Larkin steps through the curtain behind him. She looks around the little theater like she just woke up in Oz or something.

I'm so stunned to see her in my sanctuary, I don't know what to say.

Jarek starts to back out of the room. "Moby will be up in a minute. He's still . . . busy." Before he disappears through the curtain, he shoots me another wink, because I guess that's what you do when you totally betray someone.

Shelby and I size each other up in silence for a moment, then she walks down the steps to the row in front of where I'm sitting. She stands defiantly, blocking the screen.

"Maciek," she says matter-of-factly.

"Shelby."

"I've always wondered where you two disappeared to."

"It used to be a secret," I say. "How'd you get in here?"

"My friend Jarek let me in." I've managed to keep our screenings Shelby-free, despite her persistence, and now my own cousin walks her right through the front door.

"And why would he do that?"

"I told him I was meeting you here to help you."

I'm about to ask her what exactly she thinks I need *her* help with when the curtain thrashes behind me and Moby bursts into the theater.

"I wish I knew why some of them float and some sink . . . ," he begins. Then he sees Shelby and freezes like a deer trying to stay invisible to a hunter.

"Hello, Levi," she says.

Moby never moves a muscle but flicks his eyes toward me with a desperate look. He gets nervous around people he doesn't know very well, and it's even worse around girls.

"It's all right, Moby."

He walks the long way around to the other side of the row and sits next to me, never once taking his gaze off Shelby.

Moby leans in and whispers in my ear loudly enough to be heard over a chain saw. "Ask her what she wants!"

Shelby folds her arms over her chest. "Isn't it obvious? I want to join the Cadre of Evil."

Moby and I look at each other and snicker. "What the heck is the Cadre of Evil?"

Shelby looks a little bit embarrassed, but she keeps her chin high. "I'm not sure what you call your organization, but I want in."

"First of all, there is no *organization*, it's me and Moby and that's all. Second, we are not looking for new members, and there's nothing you can say that will change that."

Shelby raises an eyebrow. "Oh, really?"

I lean back in my chair and touch my fingertips together. "Really."

She reaches into her purse and pulls out a large brown envelope. "So I guess you wouldn't be interested in some embarrassing baby pictures of one Mr. Archer Norris."

Moby tugs on my arm. "Chub!" he whisper-yells at me.

I cut him off. The last thing I want to do is show Shelby how much I might want to look at those pictures. But there's a part of my brain that plans our pranks, and the pictures have switched it on. I've been searching for a way to humiliate the Arch so badly during his election speech that nobody will vote for him. If the pictures really are embarrassing, and I can project them on the wall of the gym during the Arch's speech, it could be perfect.

"You have my attention," I say as coolly as possible.

"Good," Shelby says. "I also thought the Dark Carbuncle of Doom might be a good name, or maybe—"

"First of all, I think a carbuncle is a giant zit, so that's a no. Let's see these pictures first, then maybe we'll talk names." She hands over the envelope and I open it, my hand shaking with excitement.

Shelby does not disappoint. The pictures are more embarrassing than I could've hoped. The first picture in the stack is a shot of the Arch wearing a tutu and tiara and dancing with a little girl who must be a cousin or something. The photos only get worse from there.

"Where did you get these?" I ask.

She folds her arms. "Does it matter?"

"It does to me," I say, offering the pictures back to her.

She doesn't take them.

"Grammie and I went to a yard sale at the Norrises' house. We bought some empty photo albums. Those were stuck in the back."

I tuck the envelope into my backpack and force a smile at Shelby. Then I offer my hand.

"Welcome to the organization," I say. She grins and shakes it.

I don't actually invite her to stay for the movie, but she takes a seat next to us and I don't do anything to stop her.

Just as the house lights dim, I look over at Moby. He isn't smiling the way he normally does when a movie's about to start. In fact, he doesn't look happy at all. He must still be upset about Shelby being here. I offer him some Goobers to soften him up, but he doesn't even look when I rattle the box.

I get home just in time for dinner.

Dad says grace and then forks the biggest piece of

liver onto his plate. "What was the movie?" he asks. Of course, he's already talked to Jarek and knows exactly what we saw.

"It was about owls saving the world." I grab the smallest piece of liver, knowing I will have to eat the whole thing. The truth is I didn't pay all that much attention to the movie. I was too busy figuring out ways to use my new treasure chest of resources. I drink three glasses of milk to wash the dried-out liver down my throat. It tastes like fried dirt, but the thought of ruining the Arch's campaign tastes almost sweet enough to balance it out.

My mother catches me smiling and says, "Did you have a good day at school?"

For once I don't have to exaggerate. "It was actually a really good day," I say.

My mom smiles at me, then my dad. "We had a good day at the shop, too. Very busy," she says.

"We needed a good day," my father says. "Is not easy making ends meet."

My uncle Stosh told me sausage is made of lips and buttholes, so I always assumed that was what my dad meant when he said "ends meat." Now I realize it just means paying the bills when you don't have much money, like us.

I'd rather have an extra helping of liver than hear about how things went at the shop, but I smile and act interested as I think about Mrs. Belfry's beautiful new laptop and everything I can use it for.

My dad sees me smiling and pops my bubble. "I talked to Stanislaus today. He will need help on the potato farm this summer. Good way to build character." Stanislaus is my dad's brother, Jarek's dad, who still lives in Poland. Whenever I step out of line, even a tiny bit, my dad threatens to send me there for the summer. I would rather fill my pants with ferrets than spend the summer picking potatoes in Poland.

My mom tries to change the subject. "Jarek called. He says you made a new friend today?"

Since when has Jarek become such a blabbermouth?

"I hope he is a good influence," my father says.

A half-chewed piece of liver suddenly feels like a mouthful of rubber bands. I try to answer but can't, and my mom beats me to it. "*She*," she says.

"Huh?" my dad grunts.

"Jarek said she's a girl." The corner of her mouth curls in a grin.

My dad thinks it over for a minute. I know his opinions on everything from video games to comic books to discipline, but the subject of girls has never come up. He usually dislikes things first and asks questions later, just to be safe. I prepare for the lecture I'm sure I'm about to get.

But his response shocks me. "As long as she is a good influence," he says.

They spend the rest of the meal talking about the shop and the machines they need to buy to compete against the new place a few blocks away. When my father asks how they are supposed to pay for all the new equipment, they switch to Polish for a minute. My mother forces a fake smile and says something very stern to my dad. He glances at me, and they excuse me from the table to take my bath.

"Wash your face before your *dupa*!" my mom yells after me, and I roll my eyes. She says it every time I take a bath, and it makes me feel like a little kid. I vow to myself that when I become an adult, at least once I will wash my *dupa* first.

I head upstairs, but first I stop in my parents' room to call the McQueens. If I want to pull off the prank I have in mind, I'll need their help.

CHAPTER 6

I ask the McQueens to meet me and Moby behind the Dumpsters the next day before school. We arrive five minutes early, and they're already there.

I think Delvin is wearing the hat today. "Mornin', Chub, Moby," he says, tipping the brim of the hat. "Nice day for it."

I nod to each of them. "Gentlemen," I say. "Do you think you can pull off what we talked about last night?" If they can project the baby pictures of the Arch on the wall behind him as he makes his election speech, hopefully it will shame him out of running.

I want them to start with the one of a naked three-year-old Archer grinning from ear to ear as the family cockapoo buries its face in his butt crack, and wrap up the slide show with the best shot of all: Archer wearing the same silly grin while marinating in a bathtub he's just filled with brown, trout-size turds. Why do parents feel the need to take pictures like that of their kids? No good can possibly come of it.

I'm about to make sure of that.

The hatted one pushes his lower lip out and nods. "We're up for it. Won't be easy, though."

What he really means is that it won't be cheap.

"What do you need from me to pull it off in time?"

He looks back at the other two and they all grin. They know I want this and I'm willing to pay. "Two things, Chub. The first, as always, is the proper . . . motivation."

I nod. Thanks to Mrs. Belfry's laptop, I'll be able to pay them pretty much whatever they want.

"And the second thing?"

"We get to do it our way." Their way usually

involves severe water damage and a custodian on the verge of a mental breakdown.

"Exactly how motivated will you need to be?"

"Not, sure," he says. "But this is a high-profile job, lots of exposure. It's gonna cost more than a few tardy slips."

I wince, trying to make it look like they drive a hard bargain. The truth is I'm willing to pay as much as changing a test grade from a D to a B if that's what they demand. I've looked at their files on the computer too. Darwin gets excellent grades, but Delvin and Darby have enough Ds to keep them working for me until we all graduate.

I start with a small offer. No sense giving away more than they want.

"What would you say to the disappearance of all your unexcused absences in the last term?" I ask, raising an eyebrow.

"And how do you propose to make that happen?"

"You have your methods," I say, "and I have mine."

The hat trades a quick glance with the others. They smile and nod.

"I'd say you've got yourself a deal, boyo."

I hand him the envelope containing the baby pictures. The other two come in close as he opens it.

Moby speaks up for the first time all morning. "What if we—"

I shake my head. We can't risk his input ruining another plot, not with so little time before the election.

The hatted one wipes tears of laughter from his eyes and tucks the pictures back into the envelope. "You really are evil, Chub," he says, handing the pictures to one of the others. "When these get out, the Arch might never be able to show his face in school again."

"Precisely," I purr. "Precisely."

Dad makes a lot of empty threats about a summer of potato picking in Poland. But with my anti–the Arch activity getting riskier, it's going to happen for sure if I get caught. I need an airtight alibi when things go down during the Arch's stump speech. I have to make sure I'm seen by lots of kids and teachers so they can't accuse me of having anything to do with it. This plot is much more complex than dumping a bottle of soap into a tank, so I decide to give Moby the day off too. The McQueens' services are costing enough. I'm just going to sit, make sure I'm seen so I can't be blamed, and watch the mayhem play out.

Moby and I wait for the bleachers to fill, then slowly make our way in front of the entire student body and up the stairs.

"C'mon, Chub. Let's get to our spot."

"This is different, Moby," I say out of the side of my mouth. "We want everybody to see us here."

"Why would we want that?"

As if to prove his point, someone a few rows up calls out, "Chroooome Doooooome"—a clever reference to my bald head—which gets a few chuckles.

"See?" I put my hand on his arm to slow him down. "Trust me, it's for our alibi."

Moby slows, and we make the long walk together.

Nothing to see here, folks—just a pair of normal, rule-following students going to an assembly.

Halfway across the gym we cut up into the bleachers and find a spot right in the center section on the aisle. As we sit down, I glance at Moby to make sure he's still cool. He's staring longingly at our usual spot up by the rafters.

"Trust me, Mobe."

He nods, but his leg bounces up and down with nerves.

The assembly starts right on time with Mr. Mayer leading the Pledge of Allegiance, then reminding us all to pay attention and be respectful of the candidates whether we agree with them or not. Something about him looks a little off. He doesn't have the usual spring in his step or the smile he uses when he addresses the student body. He looks tired, probably from too much late-night poker. He finishes by reminding us that it's not a popularity contest and we should vote for the person we feel will best represent our views.

I smile to myself, picturing what's about to go down. If the pictures have the right effect, this could be the first school election in history where the right person actually *does* get elected, instead of the most popular.

Sherman Mills is the first candidate to give his speech. It's more torturous than watching an adult play video games. He keeps blabbering about how we all have a responsibility to . . . something . . . something . . . something. Honestly, if a kid wants to be school treasurer so badly, I will vote for him just to get him to shut up.

Apparently, not that many kids feel like getting their butts whipped in a popularity contest today. Sherman is the only one running for treasurer, and Sam "No, I'm Really a Girl" Hardwick is the only person on the ballot for secretary. Since no one knows or cares what either of those jobs even do, it isn't difficult keeping our applause to ourselves through their speeches.

Finally it's time for the main event—the presidential speeches. Mr. Mayer steps to the podium and calls the Arch's first victim.

Rooney Filbert stumbles to the stage and pulls out a stack of papers that look like something the McQueens could use to plug an entire sewer pipe. Bored from the two speeches we've already sat through, the whole student body groans. Rooney ignores the grumbling, smooths out her ankle-length denim skirt, and proceeds to read through the document page by mind-numbing page. She lays out her 104-point plan for banning everything containing high-fructose corn syrup from the school and protecting kids with kiwi allergies from the hidden dangers lurking in our death chamber of a cafeteria. Somewhere around point seventeen (banning digitally recorded music from school dances) Moby dozes off and I catch him before he falls face-first down the ski-jump-steep stands.

The next candidate is a surprise. The crowd gasps as Mr. Mayer calls Troy Gilder up to give his speech. Troy's dark-brown hair is thick enough for a herd of elephants to hide in, which is reason enough for me to dislike him. Not to mention the fact that he is the Arch's current best friend. He's on the track team too, so I've always assumed he has Silly Putty between his ears, but I'm actually kind of impressed to discover he has an interest in something besides hair gel and mirrors. I realize my first instinct was correct, however, when he delivers his five-word speech.

"Free ice cream for everyone!" he screams, before doing the running man off the stage.

It doesn't surprise me a bit when the crowd goes wild. You don't have to be a genius to guess who's going to get the second most votes and be vice president.

"Remember, this isn't a popularity contest!" Mr. Mayer shouts into the mic, but the roar of applause drowns him out.

He waits for the hysteria to die down before he continues. "We have one more candidate left to speak. Don't forget to mark your ballot and drop it in one of the boxes in the lobby on your way out. I can't over-state the import . . . blah . . . blah . . . blah . . . your final candidate, Archer Norris."

There's another round of wild applause, which dies out when the stage stays empty. The faculty look at one another in confusion as the gym goes silent.

Have my prayers been answered? Is it possible the Arch decided not to run?

Mr. Mayer is just getting to the microphone when Nate Plemmons struts onto the stage. Nate is one of the kids the Arch hangs out with.

Nate is wearing a suit that looks like it must belong to his dad or older brother because it's way too big for him. His medium-length chestnut hair is slickly combed, and he has on a pair of dark sunglasses. He strides across the stage like a robot and stands next to the podium. A few seconds later Marlon Jenkins comes onstage dressed the same way and takes up a post opposite Nate. The two of them scan the crowd, with their hands clasped in front of them. Someone in the stands whistles and Nate tries not to laugh.

I don't know what the Arch is up to, but this shouldn't mess up what I have planned. Once the McQueens have Mr. Kraley out of the gym dealing with their plug job, and the AV club kids are distracted, they'll put up the pictures Shelby gave me and it'll be all over but the laughing.

Shelby asked to sit with Moby and me at the assembly, but it would look suspicious if a girl were suddenly sitting with us. She didn't like it, but she agreed to sit somewhere else this time. I look around now and spot her in the crowd. She winks and touches the side of her nose with her finger. I don't know if that's some code only flamingo people know or what, but she keeps doing it more forcefully until I look away.

When the crowd is back to full volume, two more kids wearing suits come onstage, followed by the future student body president.

The Arch pumps his fist in the air like he's already won the election. The crowd eats it up.

Just as he gets to the podium, someone taps me on the shoulder.

I recognize the kid's face, but I don't know his name. "Macky-sak?"

I cringe at the hatchet murder of my name. "It's Maw-check," I say slowly.

"Sorry, your dad's on the student phone. He says it's an emergency."

My first thought is that maybe Uncle Stan called from Poland to tell my dad that he'd lost the family's potato farm, but they wouldn't call me at school to tell me that. I don't want to miss the Arch's most embarrassing moment, but for my parents to call like this, it has to be super important. I follow the kid down the stairs and out to the gym's lobby, where the student phone is. As I pass through the doors, I hear the Arch say, "My fellow students, I know you all have better things to do than sit here and listen to another boring speech—" Then the doors close behind me, chopping off the rest of what he says.

The phone is on the far side of the gym's lobby, behind the tables with the ballot boxes where everyone will place their votes after the speeches. I rush to the phone, a sick feeling in my stomach.

I pick up the dangling phone. "Hello?"

"Chub?" It's not my dad. The voice on the other end of the call is filtered through some sort of electronic voice changer.

"Yes." The noise coming from the gym has changed. What was applause when the doors shut behind me now sounds more like . . . yelling.

The voice is silent. Shouts and catcalls come from the gym. Have the McQueens started the slide show without me? Even if they have, this isn't the reaction I expected. Laughter maybe, not screams.

I shout into the receiver. "Hello!"

No reply.

I look through the small window in one of the doors

to the gym. Nobody is in their seats. The assembly is out of control. Maybe the prank not only destroyed the Arch's popularity, but caused the entire popularity vortex to implode, leaving the school in chaos?

I'm about to hang up the phone and get a better look when the voice speaks again. "Have you ever played chess?"

I look at the phone and then into the gym. "Chess?" I mumble.

"Checkmate." There is a click and the line goes dead.

I drop the phone and run to the doors, but they're locked. All I can do is peer at the chaos inside.

The Arch is still on the stage, trying to keep the crowd calm. His fake Secret Service agents surround him, forming a human shield between their candidate and the crowd. The rotten-egg smell of stink bombs seeps out from under the doors.

A kid runs out of the crowd and onto the stage. His hoodie is drawn tight, and his face is covered by a grinning white mask with a pencil-thin mustache and goatee on it.

He runs toward the Arch and chucks a water balloon straight at him.

Nate dives in front of the Arch at the last second, and the balloon hits him squarely in the chest. Marlon grabs the Arch and rushes him offstage to safety as the attacker sprints out the exit at the back of the gym.

I barely have time to jump out of the way as the doors burst open and the entire student body floods out, bubbling with a mixture of glee and panic.

I bolt out of the building to the safest spot I can think of. Shelby, Moby, and two hatless McQueens arrive panting less than a minute later. Shelby pulls out an old-fashioned fan and starts fanning herself like she's having a hot flash. Moby looks totally confused. The two McQueens (Darwin and Darby, I think) just look at me and shake their heads. A second later the third McQueen sprints around the corner, holding the hat on his head to keep it from flying off as he runs.

I've never seen Shelby so happy in her life. "That . . . was . . . amazing!"

"You really outdid yourself, Chub," the third McQueen says.

It would be an amazing prank if I'd pulled it, but I didn't. Whatever just happened in there, I've been set up to take the blame.

"There's only one problem," I reply. "I didn't do any of that."

CHAPTER 7

"I lost the pictures in the stampede," the hatted triplet says. The other two stuffed wads of toilet paper in the drain holes of the drinking fountains and duct-taped down the handles, turning the west stairwell into a makeshift waterfall, to get Mr. Kraley away from the projection booth. I agree to erase half their unexcused absences and we call it even.

As soon as the deal with the McQueens is done, they disappear like a puff of smoke.

"That was quite a production," Shelby says.

"I told you, I didn't do it," I say.

Despite my denials, it's obvious she thinks I pulled

off the whole thing somehow and now I'm just being secretive about it. I consider wasting a bunch of time and energy trying to convince her it wasn't me, but instead I decide it will just be easier to ditch her and go somewhere safe to sort out my thoughts.

With everyone voting afterward, the speech assembly was my last chance to bring the Arch down before the election, and the McQueens never got the pictures up on the projector. I also need to plan for the heat that will come my way when I get framed for the riot. I can't believe I was stupid enough to fall for the fake phone call. Everyone who saw me walk in also saw me walk out right before the whole thing started.

The final bell rings while kids are still filtering through the lobby to cast their votes.

When the bell fades and the coast is clear, Moby and I head for home. Shelby follows us. Mr. Hong owns a small market we pass every day on the walk to school. His bathrooms are for paying customers only, but he makes an exception for Moby. We tell Shelby we need to do a quick pit stop, then sneak out through the window and make our escape through the alley. I don't need her trying to put in her two cents while I think.

After the Gatorade incident there's no way Mr. Mayer will let it slide if he believes I was the water balloon assassin. I can't imagine him calling the dry cleaning shop, so I figure I have at least two and a half hours left before he can get hold of my parents and they can book my flight to Poland. I could go to the shop and answer the phone all afternoon in case he calls, but if I showed up for no good reason and asked to work, my dad would know something was up. He'd make me go work on my character by pressing the pile of clothes from the mortuary that no one wants to touch.

Moby's parents are still at work, giving us plenty of time with no nosy adults asking what we're up to.

As we walk to his place, the scene inside the gymnasium keeps replaying in my head.

Like he's reading my mind, Moby says, "Who do you think did it?"

"I don't know."

"Maybe there's another kid at school who doesn't want the Arch to be president."

It's possible. I can't be the only one who wants to take the kid down a peg or two. Still, I hope Moby's wrong. When the Arch finally goes down, I want it to be my doing.

By the time we get to the Dicks' house, my mind is burning.

A wall of blue smoke boils out when we open the front door. My first thought is that the house is on fire, but Moby casually fans the smoke away and steps inside. We find the Colonel sitting in the kitchen smoking a cigar the size of a Duraflame log. He throws us a lazy salute and stubs out the handheld brush fire.

"Men," he says.

"Colonel," we respond.

"Probably best we keep the whole cigar-in-the-house thing between us, right?"

There's a smoldering tree stump in the ashtray. Mr. and Mrs. Dick would have to be wearing full scuba gear not to notice the smell.

"They won't hear it from us, sir," I say.

He nods and folds his arms over his barrel of a chest. "So what's on your minds, boys?"

I'm about to say, "Nothing," when Moby pulls out a chair opposite the Colonel, flops himself down, and proceeds to tell him exactly what just happened in amazing detail.

I don't say a word, just watch the Colonel's hard face as he takes in the story. His gigantic shaved head bobs in understanding the whole time. Moby wisely leaves out the part about us having our own plot we never got to execute.

When he finishes, the Colonel takes a deep breath and rests one of his hairy, tattooed forearms on the table. With his other arm he scratches something below the table that I'm glad I can't see. "And the assassin yelled, 'Die, milk face'?"

"It was pretty crazy in there, but I think that's what he said," Moby answers.

"Probably some Communist code. I'll ask your parents if they recognize it." He leans back in his chair and it groans under his weight. "I'd say what you boys witnessed today was what we used to call a Shanghai sucker punch."

I'm not sure I heard him correctly. "Huh?"

He puts his elbows on the table. "What I'm about to tell you men may still be classified, so this conversation never happened." He waits for us to nod before he continues. "Back in—probably shouldn't say what year, we had this General So-and-So in South—I probably shouldn't say where. Anyway, he was running for president of that little armpit of a country, and well, let's just say a certain country's government felt it would be very bad if he got elected."

"He means the United States!" Moby whispers in my ear so loud I jump.

The Colonel pretends not to hear his grandson's deafening whisper, though I'm not sure what difference it makes, since this conversation isn't officially happening.

"So we did everything we could to make sure he didn't get elected."

"And what happened?" I ask.

"During one of his campaign speeches an assassin jumped out of the crowd and shot him."

Moby gasps. "What?"

A gleam flashes in the Colonel's eye. "Everyone assumed our government sent the assassin, and because his people felt so bad for him, he won the election in a landslide. But it turned out he'd hired the assassin himself, knowing we would get blamed, which would assure him victory."

When he's done, I sit in silence, thinking about what I've just heard. Is it even possible? Were we really on the receiving end of the old Shanghai sucker punch?

If he's right, that means the Arch is now counterplotting against me. Though he doesn't have anything to get back at me for. He still has all his hair.

Then something else hits me. Why would he go through all that trouble when he knew he'd win anyway?

A chill shoots through my core when I remember him pointing at me during the assembly on Monday and pledging to "clean up this school." This is personal.

"So what happened after the election?" I ask the Colonel. "Was the general as bad as the government feared?"

A huge smile spreads across his face. "That's the best part. See, the assassin shot him in the arm so he wouldn't kill him, but he hit an artery by mistake. Old General So-and-So didn't live long enough to be sworn in. The old Shanghai sucker punch has a way of coming back to bite you."

I hope so, I think. *I hope so.*

CHAPTER 8

Mr. Mayer made it clear my free pass is over. If he believes I tried to hit the Arch with the balloon and caused the riot, it will only take one phone call to put the wheels of Polish justice in motion.

My mother walks through the door first, rubbing her lower back. She kisses me on the head. "Hello, *dynia*," she says. "How was school?"

I've been preparing myself for a grilling all day. I've decided to play it cool and make them come after me if they know something. When I open my mouth to answer, though, nerves take over. "NOTHING!"

"What this means, 'nothing'?" My father is right behind her.

My scalp flushes. *Smooth, Chub, real smooth.*

"Nothing!" I yell again.

"What is wrong with you?" My father sets down his lunchbox and looks at me.

I try to look confused and then touch my ear. "WHAT DID YOU SAY?"

My mother takes the bait. She puts her hand on my head, which is a few degrees warmer than normal because I'm so nervous. "You are warm. Maybe he has ear infection."

I do my best to look pitiful. Moms love that.

My dad backs up a few feet and points upstairs. "We can't afford to get sick."

This is better than I hoped. Now I get to sit in my room, do whatever I want, have dinner delivered, and figure out what I'm going to do when the poop hits the fan tomorrow.

The next morning I wake up early. I lay awake most of the night waiting for the phone to ring, but it never did. That means something is going to happen at school, one way or another. When I finally dozed off, it was the worst sleep of my life. I kept dreaming it was raining potatoes and the whole school was laughing at me because I was the only one they would hit. I consider playing out the ear infection story to get out of school but decide against it for two reasons:

1. I DON'T THINK I COULD SURVIVE THE WEEKEND NOT KNOWING WHAT HAPPENED AT SCHOOL.
2. LAST TIME I FAKED SICK TO GET OUT OF SCHOOL, MY DAD CAUGHT ME PLAYING TETHERBALL WITH MOBY THAT AFTERNOON AND MADE ME WORK A GARMENT PRESSER AT THE SHOP ALL WEEKEND.

I need to go to school to find out if I've been framed for the assembly riot. Someone went to a lot of trouble to make sure my alibi was ruined. The robot voice from the phone still rings in my ears. *Checkmate.*

Moby and I meet at our usual spot on the way to

school. He looks worse for wear too. "You don't look so good, Chub."

"I couldn't sleep last night."

"Me either."

Moby can fall asleep practically on command. Once, on a dare, he fell asleep while standing in line for a scoliosis check at school. He never wobbled or teetered or anything. It was kind of amazing.

"What kept you awake?" I ask.

"My parents went to their Self-Defense for Pacifists class, so the Colonel made me watch educational programming all night," he said.

"Civil War tactics again?"

"*Apocalypse Preppers.*"

We walk in silence for a while, both of us too frazzled from lack of sleep for small talk.

We're a half block from school when a shadow hits my shoulder. Shelby is wearing a wool cape over her shoulders. One gigantic button holds it in place around her noodle neck.

We stop and face her stare. "Wow, you guys must've

been pretty constipated!" She folds her arms. "Maybe you should put a little dish soap in your drinks to help move things along."

I forgot we told her we had to go to the bathroom before ditching her yesterday.

"Shelby—" I start to say.

She waves a finger in my face. "Friends don't ditch friends." Then she turns the finger around and pushes her glasses back up her nose.

I consider explaining the whole thing about the Shanghai sucker punch and throwing in a line about my terrible ear infection to soften her up a little, but I can see in her eyes she's really hurt.

"And please don't make any lame excuses." Her lip quivers. "People always have reasons why they aren't there when you need them, Maciek. I thought we were a cadre."

I come dangerously close to apologizing, when a better thought comes to me.

I do my best to look embarrassed. "I probably should've told you about rule five," I say.

She puts a finger behind her glasses and wipes her eye. "What's rule five?"

"Rule five is our escape protocol. If we are ever in real trouble, we split up and don't tell each other where we're going," I say.

"Let me get this straight. You didn't even have a name for the cadre until two days ago, but you have rules?"

"It's more of a guideline, really."

"Why don't you tell each other?" she asks.

I'm surprised at how easily the made-up explanation comes out of my mouth. "That way if one person gets caught by a teacher or something, he can't turn in the other."

She thinks about it for a moment. "I don't like that rule. Cadres are better off together, *especially* when they're in trouble."

"The other rule is new members don't get to vote on rules. Right, Moby?" I say, turning to him.

I should've known Moby would be long gone.

Hundred-year-old buildings are always creepy, but today, with no idea what's waiting for me inside, Alanmoore looks downright scary. It looms over me, appearing way taller than just four stories.

The chatter of kids is deafening as I push open the old wooden doors of the main entrance. In the halls, yesterday's assembly is all anyone is talking about. I keep my head down as I push through a crowd of kids, managing to avoid my locker and make it to homeroom without running into Mr. Mayer. Mr. Funk comes into the room after the second bell rings.

He gets to his desk and dumps an armload of books and loose papers on it. "All right, everyone, keep it down," he says, despite the fact that nobody is even talking.

At exactly 8:01 Mr. Mayer's voice crackles over the loudspeaker. "Good morning, Alanmoore," he says without his usual enthusiasm. "The chess team will be holding their annual blah . . . blah . . . blah . . ." I look over at Shelby. She still has her arms folded, and her glasses magnify her death-ray glare. I don't think she bought the rule-five thing. Whatever her deal is, she's not letting it go.

Moby sneaks into the room after Mr. Funk is sitting at his desk. He avoids eye contact with both of us. *What's that about?*

"Blah . . . blah . . . election results . . . blah." The words grab my attention and a hot rush goes through me. This is it—time to find out if the Shanghai sucker punch worked out better for the Arch than it did for ol' General So-and-So.

The two positions no one cares about are no surprise. Sam Hardwick is the new student body secretary, and Sherman Mills is our treasurer. If I ever need to dictate a letter or borrow a gold doubloon, I'll know who to call.

Then it's time to hear the names of our new leaders. I flick my eyes at Rooney Filbert. She's clutching her 104-point plan to her chest like a good-luck token.

"C'mon, Rooney!" I say under my breath. Maybe, just maybe, enough kids decided to vote for someone who actually cares about real issues instead of just the most popular kid.

"Your VP is Troy Gilder."

One kid in the back of the class tries to start a slow clap, but it doesn't catch.

Please, student body, don't let me down.

"And your student body president is . . . Archer Norris."

You know that thing in movies where somebody suddenly realizes something that changes the world as he knows it, and the background pulls away as the camera zooms in on him real fast?

Well, that doesn't happen to me.

It doesn't happen to you when middle school just keeps on disappointing you like it always has.

Slow Clap tries again, and this time it catches on. Mr. Funk looks up over the edge of his newspaper, shakes his head, and goes back to reading.

The hallways echo with applause from all over the school. Then it fades, and Mr. Mayer says, "Alanmoore Middle School, welcome your new student body president—Archer Norris."

"Friends, fellow students, Kangaroos." The Arch sounds even more smug than normal. "You have spoken and I've heard your cries."

"Keep it short, Archer," says Mr. Mayer in the background.

"So in summaration, let me say this. Most of you will not regret voting for me, and let the Norristocracy begin!"

There's more applause, mostly from jocks, I assume. Everyone else is probably busy trying to figure out the meaning of the big words our illustrious leader just invented.

Mr. Funk folds his paper and calls the class to order. I don't hear a word he says as I stare out the window at the teachers' parking lot. Outside, to my surprise, the world looks pretty much like it did yesterday. The only thing that's new is Mr. Kraley talking to himself and wandering in big, random loops in the parking lot. The poor guy looks like he hasn't slept in a week. Maybe I need to have the McQueens cool it for a while.

At lunchtime I stop by my locker to grab the books I need for the rest of the day. A note falls to the ground when I open the door. I unfold it and catch a whiff of fried potatoes. There's a smudge on one corner I can only hope is ketchup.

Want the truth? Boys' room, 4th floor, lunch.

It could be a trap, but I smile at what it might mean if it isn't.

I quickly track down the McQueens and enlist them as security. They aren't all muscly like the Arch, but together they aren't scared of anyone, and I'm pretty sure the three of them can handle anybody at the school. I don't want to scare away the potential informant, but I'm not going to walk into a trap without any backup, either. As the rest of the kids flood down the stairs to the cafeteria, we work our way upstream to the fourth floor.

I give them instructions not to scare away the mystery note writer, and then one of the triplets slowly opens the door to the bathroom and slips inside. A moment later he returns and signals the all clear. The three of them stand watch by the door as I go inside.

The bathroom appears empty. The only light in the room comes through the high window on the far side. My steps echo off the tile walls. If the anonymous note writer is in here, he's in one of the stalls.

The doors of the first two are open. The third stall is empty too except for a ten-pound mud weasel someone forgot to flush. I think of Moby disappearing earlier, then sliding into homeroom after the bell. I slam the door before the weasel comes to life and attacks me.

The fourth stall has no door. It's under repairs, and has been forever, which leaves the one against the far wall.

I stand outside the door. "Ahem!"

A fake, high voice replies. "Occupied."

What now? I try again. "AHEM!"

"Can you pass me some paper?" says the voice.

I'm getting annoyed. Why wouldn't you check to make sure there's paper before you sit down? That's a lesson you learn the first time you have to poop at school.

I pull out the note to make sure I read it properly. Yep, definitely the right place at the right time.

"*Any* piece of paper will work."

I look at the note and realize what the bad Kermit the Frog impersonator is asking. I fold it back up and flick it under the stall.

Apparently, it does the trick, because a second later the door creaks open.

It is *a trap!* Julius Jackson steps out of the stall. *How could I have been so stupid?*

He stands more than a full head taller than me, and he's so wide he fills up the stall's doorway. When you think of Alanmoore track, you think of Julius Jackson—or at least you did, until the Arch joined the team. Everyone calls him Sizzler, partly because he's the fastest kid in school, but mainly because he usually has enough food stuck in his braces to open his own all-you-can-eat buffet.

I fight back my nerves. "Did you leave me the note?"

He nods.

"Is this a trap?" I say. There's no reason for him to lie to me. If it is a trap and I try to run, he'll be all over me before I can even call for help.

For such a fast guy he talks very slowly. "No trap," he says.

"Why am I here, then?"

"Cuz you know the Arch has no interest in being

student body president and you want to know what he's really up to."

Maybe someone else in this school is paying attention. "I'm listening."

Sizzler shuffles from foot to foot and jams his hands into his pockets.

I turn for the door. "Drop me another note when you've got something to say."

"*He* planned it," he says quietly.

I stop.

"The speech, the fake assassination—he planned all of it."

"The Shanghai sucker punch," I say through gritted teeth.

"He had the principal's permission for the Secret Service thing. The water balloon part was extra. You know how he is."

I know how he is, all right. He's the kind of kid who never gets in trouble for taking things too far because even adults think he's perfect.

"Anyway, there was no way he could've known everyone would go nuts like that. He just wanted to make sure it was a speech nobody would ever forget."

I look down as I run through what happened. *Permission?* That explains why there wasn't a phone call last night. "But there were stink bombs."

Sizzler laughs. "No one can prove Archer's guys lit those. It got a little out of hand, but hey, it got people talking. Everyone knows you can't stand him since . . ."

I whip my head up and glare at Sizzler. I don't need to be reminded about *the incident*.

"Since second grade," he continues. "You try to embarrass him every chance you get. Archer knew everyone would assume *you* were behind the water balloon, and when Nate and Marlon stopped it, he'd be more popular than ever. You have to admit, it was pretty cool."

I take a step toward him. The light through the window behind him makes his Afro look like a halo. I tell myself it must be a pain having that much hair, but who am I kidding? I'd take it if I could.

Since he's so talkative, I ask, "Why go to all the trouble? He would've been elected anyway."

"He wanted to be SURE he'd get elected. He got

you out of the gym so everyone would think it was you with the water balloon."

"He wants to get rid of me that badly?"

On one hand, it makes me nervous that the Arch is now so focused on my destruction. On the other hand, it means that all my efforts haven't gone unnoticed. I smile at the idea that I'm getting under his skin.

"That's what I'm here to tell you," Sizzler says. "It's not even about you. He's in some kind of trouble."

This might be worth missing lunch for after all. "What kind of trouble?"

"Dunno, but it's like his life depends on it or something."

That sounds crazy, but if it's true, it must be something serious. The Archer I knew never got steamed up about anything.

"So why are you telling me this? Because now that he's on the track team, you aren't Coach Farkas's favorite?"

He deflates a little, and I know I've nailed it. He looks like he might cry, but he just says, "Track's the only thing I'm good at. I work hard at it because I love it."

"So you want him taken down because he's faster than you?"

He shakes his head. "Don't you get it? Archer doesn't care about the track team. It's easy for him, so it doesn't mean anything to him. When we leave Alanmoore, he'll forget all about the track team. This was my year to do something special. Doesn't seem fair."

I almost tell him I understand exactly how he feels, but the boys' room, marinating in the smell of Moby's gluten-free turd, doesn't seem like the place for a group hug. Best to keep it all business.

"What kind of secret could he have that he needs to become student body president to cover it up?"

He shrugs his broad shoulders. "I just thought you should know, since you're the only one who isn't under his spell."

"And you are hoping I'll help you figure out what he's hiding and get your spot back."

He's embarrassed to look me in the eye now that I've figured out his angle, so I let him off the hook. "Good. You came to the right place."

This is important info, and I should offer Julius something for it: a changed grade, an erased tardy, maybe a toothpick?

"So what do you want?" I ask. He shrugs again, and suddenly a thought occurs to me. This is my chance to get something more valuable than one little scrap of information. This is my chance to get my own spy in the Arch's circle. "Are you and Archer on good terms?"

"I guess, but if anyone finds out I talked to you, everyone will probably hate me."

I tent my fingers. "Julius, do you know what a cadre is?"

Then I explain to him what I want him to do.

He shakes his head as I talk. "I dunno, Mazi . . . sack."

I wave my hand. "Please, call me Chub."

"I dunno, Chub. It seems kind of . . . illegal or something."

"Look, Sizzler," I say. "If we're going to let you into the cadre, we need to know you aren't secretly working with the Arch. You have to do this to prove it, see?"

Sizzler thinks about it for a moment. He needs a nudge.

"You came to me, remember? If I turn you away, do you think you can go back to being one of his mindless followers?" I wait for him to do the math.

"I guess not," he says.

"Then you know what you have to do."

After a moment he nods, sticks his hands in his pockets, and slowly walks out of the bathroom.

Maybe Shelby is right. Maybe having a cadre can be useful after all.

CHAPTER 9

Lunchtime is almost over. Rather than risk a run-in with the Arch or any members of his Secret Service, I decide to wait in the abandoned stairwell behind the library for the bell to ring. I need some time to make sense of what Sizzler told me. The Arch being in big trouble is good news, so why does it make me nervous?

The door to the stairwell is in the back of Mrs. Belfry's office. She's in her chair, as still as a statue, and for a split second I wonder if she's been filed in the great card catalog in the sky. She's sitting bolt upright with her hands folded in front of her on the desk.

I'm not an expert or anything, but I have seen a dead body before. My parents made me look at my uncle Stosh in the casket at his funeral (it's a Polish thing; don't ask). I was nervous about it until I actually saw him. When Uncle Stosh was alive, his favorite hobby was mining for gold—in his nose. Decades of burrowing for boogers, or "picking winners" as he used to call it, left him with nostrils big enough to hangar a blimp. Whoever got him ready for the casket had decided to *fix* his nostrils by flattening them back to a normal size. When I figured out what looked weird about him, my anxiousness disappeared and I could even laugh, but only because Stosh would have thought it was funny too. My parents, however, didn't think it was funny, and that weekend I got to learn how to run a single-buck vacuum shirt press.

Mrs. Belfry's nostrils look pretty lifelike, but I pause by the door for a minute to make sure I don't need to call 911. I'm about to look for a mirror to hold under her nose when she sucks in a gasping snort. *She might just make it to two hundred after all.* I slip through the forgotten door and close it behind me as quietly as possible.

The stairway is my little secret. It goes from the library on the fourth floor all the way to the basement, where the old steam boilers heat the water for the radiators. I discovered it during a detention, and I've used it several times for escapes and shortcuts, or just when I need a place to get away. I don't see Mr. Mayer sitting on one of the steps until I almost trip over him.

He doesn't seem all that surprised to see me. "Maciek."

My eyes are adjusting to the dark, but I glimpse the telltale glow of a cell phone's screen as he shoves it in his pocket.

I stay on the step just above him. "Mr. Mayer." The stairway isn't technically off-limits, since nobody knows it exists. Still, I wait for him to say something first.

He lets out a deep sigh. "How much of that did you overhear?"

The truth is I was so wrapped up in my own

thoughts, I didn't hear a word of his conversation, but instinct tells me not to admit that.

"Enough?" I say, not *technically* lying.

Mr. Mayer hangs his head. He doesn't talk for almost a minute.

I don't move a muscle.

"Then you know this isn't good."

A giant bubble forms and then pops in my stomach. He was on the phone with my parents and I've stupidly wandered into his little ambush. My mind scrambles through my options. How long will it take my parents to replace my passport if I'm able to find it and burn it? It probably won't get me out of my trip to prison planet Poland. My dad will just figure out a way to put me in a box and ship me as freight.

"You're a smart kid. You apply it in odd ways, but you're smart. What would you do if you were me?" he asked.

Maybe Sizzler was wrong. Maybe the Arch didn't have permission for the riot and Mr. Mayer does think I'm responsible. Will he really give me the chance to decide my own discipline? "I guess an act of mercy is out of the question?" I say.

He laughs. "That would be nice, but this is a lot more serious than that."

The stomach bubble rises again. It doesn't matter that I'm innocent this time, I'm going to pay one way or another, just like the Arch planned.

I'm about to throw myself on Mr. Mayer's mercy and tell him everything I know when he turns to face me. His eyes are red. Pushing the boundaries is one thing, but making an adult cry is a line you don't want to cross. My knees shake.

"Mr. Mayer, I'm—"

"You know what, I shouldn't be talking to you about this," he says, standing up and dusting off his pants. "In fact, I think it's best if neither of us ever brings *it* up again."

I'm starting to wonder if we are having the same conversation.

"There's a lesson in this, though," he says.

I don't want him to clam up because I sense he's

about to give me something good. "Mmm-hmm," I mumble.

He puts his hand on my shoulder. "Don't ever gamble more than you can afford to lose."

"Mmm," I say, trying to sound like I'm pondering this pearl of wisdom, even though I still have no clue what the heck he's babbling about. Honestly, do adults really believe kids know or care what they mean when they say stuff like that? Gambling? Seriously, does he think—

Suddenly a trapdoor springs open in my mind. He isn't talking about the riot at all. He's talking about the other thing that only he and I know about—*poker*!

That's why he's talking on the cell phone in the secret stairwell. He can't risk anyone overhearing him discussing his little hobby.

I need him to give me more. This info could be very useful, especially now that it looks like I'm going to be covering up for a whole bunch of people, not just Moby and me. I nudge him to spill the good stuff. "What are you going to do?"

He shakes his head. "The only thing I *can* do. Figure out how to beat this Mr. X and play my way out of this hole."

This is officially too good to be true. One minute I think I'm getting deported for a crime I didn't commit, the next my principal is giving me enough dirt on him to guarantee me a free ride through school. The mess he's in explains why he never even asked me about the assembly.

"And Mr. X is . . ."

"He's the whole reason I'm in this mess. I was almost qualified for the regional poker tournament when he started showing up at our league nights and winning games I had in the bag. I thought it was a fluke at first, but he just keeps winning and winning. I was sure I could figure out his game, but it's impossible."

I don't want him to get sidetracked, because it's all actually pretty interesting. "What makes him so hard to figure out?"

"He wears these sunglasses and a big cowboy hat. Not to mention his mustache, which covers half his face. It makes him impossible to read."

I start to think how unfair it is that someone

would get extra hair on his face when some of us don't even have it on our heads, but I catch myself and try to figure out what I would do if I were Mr. Mayer. "So why don't you just not play him anymore?"

He sighs. "I wish it were that simple. Now that we're almost in the qualifier, I have to play him to get in. The real problem is I can't afford to sit out now. I've dug myself a pretty big hole with Mace, trying to take this guy down."

I haven't heard that name before. "Who's Mace?"

"He lends me money. He's what's called a loan shark. He's the one who I was on the phone with when you . . ."

The confusion must show on my face, because Mr. Mayer stops talking and lets out a deep sigh.

He's suddenly unable to look me in the eye. "You didn't overhear the call at all, did you?"

I shrug and try to look apologetic, but it's hard to mask my outright glee at that moment. I had a little bit of dirt on Mr. Mayer before, but he's just unloaded a dump truck full of it in my front yard.

Mr. Mayer tells me he feels sick, so I leave him in

the stairwell and make my way to the basement, then back up the other stairs to Mr. Kraley's utility room. I feel a lot better about things as I push open the door that leads out toward the Dumpsters.

Now that I know Mr. Mayer is in no position to worry about what I'm up to, I need to get the cadre together to start planning the Arch's impeachment. Yes sir, things look pretty good compared with the way the day started. That is, until a hand lands on my shoulder.

Marlon and Nate are still dressed in the oversize suits and sunglasses they wore at the assembly when they "rescued" the Arch from the fake assassination.

"Mr. Turbo-Chunky," Marlon says. "Please come with us."

"What? Where?"

Nate Plemmons kicks my feet apart and starts patting me down like I'm being arrested. "*He* wants to see you," Nate says.

I slap Nate's hand away and dust myself off. Some kids see what's happening and quickly look the other way, not wanting to get involved.

Marlon puts a hand on my shoulder and nudges me toward the gym. I stop walking and stare at his hand, and after a few seconds of standoff he lets go of me and points the way.

CHAPTER 10

I should have expected this, but it's happening sooner than I would've guessed and with a lot less subtlety. Nate and Marlon lead me into the locker room, then back away and stand by the door. I roll my eyes, but they just stare back blankly from behind their matching sunglasses. I'm trying to think of something clever to say when the Arch's voice echoes off the brick walls.

"Nice of you to join me."

I turn. He's standing on top of the half wall that separates the showers from the rest of the locker room.

My heart feels like a woodpecker trying to beat its

way through my rib cage. "Nice of you to send your flying monkeys to give me a ride," I say. *Not bad.*

"Whatever." He paces back and forth like a cat walking a fence. "Do you know why you're here?"

The end-of-lunch bell rings.

"No," I say. "But you better make it quick. We're gonna be late for class."

"Oh, maybe you didn't hear the news. I'm student body president now."

"*Yeah*," I say as sarcastically as possible. "I'm pretty sure you still have to go to class."

"We'll see, we'll see." He strokes his chin.

"Well, maybe you don't have to go to class, but I do, so . . ." I turn to leave and the fake Secret Service agents step forward to block my way.

I sigh. I have zero chance of bulling my way past these two. They have me outmatched in almost every way.

"Besides," the Arch says, "if you didn't get in trouble for the assembly, I doubt you'll get in trouble for missing a few minutes of math."

I don't want this meeting to last any longer than

it has to. He is the student body president now and I am the known troublemaker, so my odds of getting busted for being late are way higher than his. And I don't want to waste my new info on Mr. Mayer on something as trivial as a one-class tardy. "Well, you seem to have all the answers. Why don't you guys just beat me up or whatever you're gonna do, so I can go?"

The Arch lets out a laugh. "You think I brought you here to beat you up?"

Suddenly I'm embarrassed. The truth is I'm scared of what they might do to me, but I shouldn't throw myself at their feet so easily.

"If you're not going to beat me up, then why am I here?"

"You're here because I'm the president now, and somehow you have a way of conveniently getting out of trouble with Mr. Mayer. Whether I like it or not, that makes you and me the two most powerful people in this school."

Taking a compliment from him is like winning a Nickelodeon award—flattering, but you end up dripping with slime after you get it.

He stops pacing. "I thought you were a genius," he says. "Do I really have to spell it out for you?"

I'm not going to give him anything for free. Whatever he wants, he's going to have to say it.

"I guess you do."

"I called you here to offer a truce."

I'd be lying if I said I don't feel a tiny bit of relief at his words. Is this the moment I've been hoping for all these years? Is he about to apologize and go back to being plain old Archer Norris? I glance over my shoulder at his bodyguards and make a mental note to ask the Colonel how many times someone has been kidnapped and dragged to a secret room to negotiate a peace treaty. Something smells funny, and it isn't just the laundry cart full of sweaty track uniforms.

"Do we need the goons here to talk about a truce?"

The Arch thinks for a moment, snaps his fingers, and points to the door. Like a pair of well-trained Dobermans, Marlon and Nate give me one last sneer apiece and shuffle out, leaving the Arch and me alone in the locker room.

As the echo of the slamming door fades, the Arch

hops down and looks me in the eye. The cocky mask that everyone at Alanmoore knows as his signature look melts away, and he takes a few steps toward me so we're only feet apart. My heart races.

"C'mon, Chub, why do we have to fight? Why can't we just get along, like . . ." He trails off and looks at the ground.

I want to make him say it. I want him to choke on the words. "Like what, Archer?"

"Why can't we just get along like . . . we did when we were friends?"

I run a hand over my bald scalp. "Because you've changed. And so have I."

Archer Norris plops down on one of the benches and looks up at me. I search his face for a glimmer of the kid who used to be my best friend. The kid I used to spend weekends with, reading comics in the fort we built in the woods behind his house. He looks away and stares at the painted concrete floor. "That was a long time ago. Don't you think it's time we put that aside? What are you hoping to accomplish by being such a weirdo, anyway?"

I suddenly feel bold. "What are *you* trying to accomplish by being such a jerk?"

He's quiet for a moment. "I'm just acting the way people expect me to act."

I flinch. This is not at all what I was expecting him to say. I know what it's like having people treat you a certain way because of your size and how you look.

But then I remember what Sizzler said, about how the Arch *needs* to be president, about how he has something major to hide.

"I guess that's the difference between us, then," I say. "I don't do anything because people expect me to, and I don't pretend to be something I'm not."

He shakes his head, still staring at the ground. Is the fact that he threw away our friendship finally sinking in?

"So as long as you keep being *the Arch* for everyone else, we can't go back to the way it was."

My pulse rushes in my ears. Even though I can't imagine him beating me up himself, the possibility of Archer summoning his goons to pound me into pudding still exists. He stands up and faces me, his eyes narrowing.

He's wearing the Arch mask again.

"I was afraid you'd say something like that," he says, and hops up on the bench and then up onto the wall so he's looking down at me.

He fumbles in his pocket for something.

"I gotta say, Chub, I'm pretty disappointed in you." He finds what he was looking for in his pocket and pulls it out, flipping open the spout on a little yellow bottle and spraying a clear liquid onto the pile of uniforms in the laundry cart. I catch a whiff of the liquid as he puts the bottle back in his pocket. It smells like the stuff my dad uses to light the barbecue. Then the Arch pulls a silver lighter from his other pocket and flicks it to life.

"A truce could've been good for both of us."

I glance at the pile of clothes, then at the flame.

"But this time you've really gone too far."

Before I can yell "*NOOOOO*," he tosses the lighter into the pile of uniforms. A wicked blue flame bursts up and spreads like lava spilling out of a volcano.

Every fire safety tip I've ever learned disappears, and I run back and forth in raw panic.

Black smoke curls off the melting uniforms and up to the ceiling. I'm paralyzed watching the fire when a hand grips my arm. The Arch drags me away from the fire and out the door into the main courtyard.

When we're safely outside in the fresh air, I realize I'm still holding my breath. He lets go of my arm and I drop to my knees, drawing in a lungful of the good stuff. For some reason I'm about to thank him, but I stop myself as I look up. His face is pure, cocky Arch, not the look of someone who is about to be kicked out of school for arson. What the heck just happened in there? What could he possibly have to gain by burning up his own track team's uniforms right after he won the election?

Footsteps echo off the brick breezeway. My scalp starts to sweat when I look up and see Nate and Marlon sprinting toward us, with Mr. Mayer close behind.

CHAPTER 11

Thankfully, Mr. Kraley quickly put out the fire with an extinguisher, but not before it turned the pile of uniforms into a giant black puddle of goo.

Mr. Mayer marches me back to his office in silence, the kind of silence adults use when they are beyond angry. He pushes me toward my usual seat and slams the door behind us.

"Mr. Mayer," I say, not sure what I'm going to say next.

"If I were you, Maciek, I'd just keep quiet right now." He goes on his laptop and searches something.

I'm smart enough to know what this looks like.

Everyone knows I have an ax to grind with the Arch. It looks like I went crazy after he won the election and burned the track uniforms as revenge. Even though it's my word against the Arch's about what happened in the locker room, I need to say something to soften Mr. Mayer up a little before he calls my dad.

"I didn't do it!" I say as he picks up the receiver.

He blows air through his lips, shakes his head, and dials the number he's found on the laptop.

"Mr. Trzebiatowski? This is Principal Mayer. I hate to bother you at work, sir, but . . . No, everyone is fine, but I need you to come to the school as soon as you can. There's been a . . . an incident."

My head burns imagining what my father is thinking as he hears those words. My parents work really hard just to afford the cheapest house in the school district. Whether I'm guilty or not, having to leave work to deal with this will mean punishment for me.

He hangs up the phone and sighs. I figure he'll start suspension paperwork right now, but he just sits in his chair rubbing his forehead while we wait.

How did this all go so wrong? My campaign

against the Arch used to be like chess, now it's becoming more like chain saw juggling.

My dad arrives ten minutes later. Mr. Mayer tells me to wait in the outer office, and the two of them go into Mr. Mayer's office and shut the door, leaving me alone with Mrs. Osborne. She works on some papers on her desk, avoiding eye contact.

After an eternity the door opens again, my dad marches past me, and I get up. Mr. Mayer stands in the doorway rubbing his temples. The hair there is a lot grayer than it was just a few weeks ago. I'm not sure if it's me or this Mace character making him age so fast, but if Mr. Mayer has a rope, he looks like he's at the end of it.

I search his face, desperate for a clue to my fate.

"We'll deal with this on Monday," he says, and then disappears into his office.

I almost apologize, but catch myself. What am I thinking? The Arch did this, not me. As though he hasn't made things hard enough for me, now he's about to get me kicked out of school for something *he* did.

The ride home is silent—outer-space silent, which makes it worse. At least if my dad tore off a chunk of my butt, I'd know where I stand. But chewing butt cheek like a lion feasting on a gazelle is what you do when you are angry. He's something way worse than angry—he's disappointed.

Most kids have it easy dealing with a disappointed parent. The parent will say something like, "I expect better decisions from you, Johnny." Then Johnny nods apologetically and they go eat meat loaf for dinner.

It's different for me. When immigrant parents are disappointed, you get to hear the whole story of how they came to America with nothing but a dream. Every time you disappoint them, the story gets worse and you feel more and more guilty. Trust me, nobody can use guilt better than parents who crossed an ocean to give *you* a better life.

I want to say something to defend myself, but my dad's white-knuckle grip on the steering wheel of our old car tells me I'm better off exercising my right to remain silent. Whatever I say right now can and will be used against me somehow.

When we drive past our house, I know what Dad has in store for me. I guess it doesn't matter to him that I haven't technically been charged with setting the uniforms on fire, and Mr. Mayer isn't going to do anything until he figures out what actually happened. Without even standing trial, I'm getting sentenced to a weekend of hard labor.

Fridays are busy at the dry cleaning shop, especially in the spring and summer. Tons of people come in Friday afternoon to pick up clothes for weekend weddings or to drop off clothes they want cleaned for the next week at the office. I know there's no shortage of character-building in store for me. With the workout I'm bound to get, my character will be pumped up like a bodybuilder by the time I go back to school on Monday.

Dad parks in the alley behind the shop and pushes me in through the back door. The Friday rush is in full swing up front. I take off my coat to go help my mom with the customers, but Dad stops me with a hand on my shoulder. The only two words he says to me all day sound like the title of a horror film as he growls them under his breath. "The Pile."

He lets go of my shoulder and heads up front to help my mom.

The Pile is a mountain of filthy old clothes donated by funeral parlors and people who don't want them stinking up their own houses anymore. We take them in, and whenever my parents have spare time (or slave labor), they clean them and give them to local charities. My sentence is to sort the usable clothes from the trash and get the ones that can be saved ready to be cleaned.

I haven't been to the shop since last week, and I hope someone else has worked on the Pile a little bit since my last run-in with the law.

No such luck. The Pile is even bigger than the last time I saw it, a life-size cotton, wool, and polyester statue of Jabba the Hutt. The only difference is it's not Princess Leia chained to it, it's a little Polish kid, a.k.a. me.

I don't want to get caught standing around when my dad comes back, so I roll up my sleeves and get to work. I pick up an old tweed blazer and inspect it for damage. The blazer was acting as a seal between the earth's atmosphere and the reservoir of stink that lives in the Pile, so removing the seal releases a smell like rotten meat mixed with a walrus fart. My T-shirt over my nose does very little to keep me from gagging. I briefly feel bad for making Moby marinate in Mr. Kraley's BO in the kangaroo suit, but there's at least a weekend's worth of work ahead of me, and there's no time for getting all weepy when you're working the Pile.

When I was a little kid, I used to love going to my parents' shop. Back then, before Archer turned himself into the Arch, he and I used to go to the shop on weekends to run the garment carousel and get plastic bags to make parachutes for our G.I. Joes. When we were little, the Pile was better than a jungle gym. My dad always told us to stay away from it or we'd regret it, but whenever he was distracted, we would climb on it and burrow under it like it was a giant pile of raked-up leaves.

At the end of our first week of second grade a rumor spread through the school like wildfire. Someone had brought lice to school, and the next day every student's scalp would be inspected. Nobody wants to be known as the kid who gave the school lice. Once you are *that* kid, you'll never be known for anything else until you grow up and move away.

I didn't want to believe it, but I knew it was us. That day after school Archer and I met behind the shed where they kept the school's sports equipment. Neither of us wanted to say what we were both thinking.

"We should see if it's us," I said.

"What do we do if it is?" Archer said.

My dad stored extra chemicals for the shop at home, and I knew there were some bottles of stuff he used to kill lice when they found them in the Pile, which was all the time. If we could kill our own lice before the inspection tomorrow, we'd be clear and no one would know it was us that had infected the school.

A plan was forming in my mind. "I think I know what to do."

Archer trusted me. "Okay."

When we got to my basement, we decided we should make sure we actually had lice before we started pouring chemicals all over each other.

"You want to go first?" I said.

"I guess so." He leaned over and I looked at his hair. I had no idea what lice even looked like, but I figured it would be obvious if I saw one. He had some dandruff, but none of it was moving. I was about to tell him he was all clear when I saw first one, then hundreds of the little monsters on his scalp.

I jumped back like I'd been stung and watched the hope fade from my best friend's face.

Then he checked me, and my worst second-grade fears came true too.

Archer was taller, so I held the chair as he grabbed the bottle of lice killer off the top shelf. We were desperate, and the picture of the dead bug on the label was good enough for us.

"How do you do it?" Archer asked. I guess it never occurred to us to read the label. Let me tell you, if I could go back, I would make myself read that label.

"My dad just sprays it on the clothes."

We rock-paper-scissored for it, and as usual Archer won.

My hair, when I had some, was curly and blond. The kind of hair old ladies loved to touch, then say things like "If I had those curls . . ."

I parted it with my fingers so Archer could spray the stuff straight onto my scalp. I don't know how much he sprayed on there, but my hair was dripping with it when he was done.

I went to take the bottle to spray him, too, but he held it out of reach.

He studied my dripping mop of hair. "Let's make sure it works first." The stuff smelled like gasoline and Lysol, which probably should've been a clue.

After a minute he asked, "Does it feel like it's working?"

"I don't know. How do . . ." But before I could finish my sentence, my head felt like it had caught fire, killing all the lice in a single, flaming instant. It was like a million little lice voices crying out in agony, and then they were suddenly silenced.

I stuck my head under the faucet until the burning cooled. When I stood up, I wasn't on fire anymore, but my eyes were full of tears. I gingerly touched my head and hoped. The pain would have been worth it if all the lice were dead. But when I looked at my hand, my heart almost stopped. I was clutching a knot of tight blond curls.

Archer's face was pale. We'd borrowed a mirror from my mom's room, and he clutched it to his chest.

"Does it look bad?" I asked, although I could read the answer in the horrified look on his face.

He just stood there with his mouth open, staring.

I growled in frustration and held out my hand. "Mirror!"

"What?" He started backing away, like he was suddenly scared of me.

"Hand me the mirror!"

He didn't want to hand it over, so I pulled it out of his hands.

When I saw what the stuff had done, I knew why he didn't want me to see.

For the first time in my life when I looked at my

own face, it wasn't trimmed with golden curls. My scalp was red and raw, like the worst sunburn ever. Other than a few stubborn clumps of hair that fell out later, I was completely bald.

After Archer left the basement, everything was different. The next day he lined up for lice check like everyone else. It was no surprise that he had them, and he got sent home with a bottle of lice-killing shampoo.

It didn't take long for the kids at school to blame the breakout on the kid who'd had a full head of hair one day and was bald the next. I thought about trying to explain it to everyone. About how it wasn't me, it was *us*—me and my best friend, Archer. I wanted everyone to know it was a simple mistake and it wasn't because people with accents carried strange diseases. Of course, it would've meant something only if Archer had stood up and vouched for my story. But something changed in him when he saw my hair fall out. He could've stood by me, but he didn't want any part of the taunting and teasing and pointing and laughing I endured when I showed up at school bald. That day everyone stopped looking at me as the quiet little Polish kid, and suddenly I became the bald foreign freak who'd given the school lice. But the worst part wasn't even the teasing, it was that my best friend acted like he didn't even know me.

And that's why I've got to bring Archer down.

CHAPTER 12

I'm pretty sure every weekend has the same number of hours in it. So why does one spent reading comic books and watching TV seem to fly by, but a weekend on the Pile feels like ten years?

I reckon I can sort the entire thing by the time we close on Saturday, but I don't want to give my dad a chance to come up with something worse for me to do on Sunday. My uncle Stosh once said, "Better the devil you know than the devil you don't." I think this is the kind of situation he was talking about. This devil has a horrible case of BO, but at least I can't smell it after the first hour. No telling what might be in store with the next devil. Then again, I also overheard Stosh saying that to a freshly picked booger the size of a cornflake, so maybe I'm reading too much into it.

The trick to enduring this punishment is to finish up the Pile at the exact same time my dad is ready to go home. If I finish early, he'll just come up with some fresh horror for me to deal with. But if I leave any part of it unsorted, I'll end up right back here next weekend. I have to time it just right.

By noon on Sunday I feel like one of those marathon runners who poop their pants and have to get an IV after they crawl across the finish line. I haven't even glanced at a comic book all weekend, and I'm having pretty severe TV withdrawal too. If I *had* played any part in the uniform fire, I probably would've learned my lesson by now and vowed to change my ways. However, I'm clearly the prime suspect and will probably get deported for something the Arch did, so the whole thing just makes me more determined than ever to take him down. I have no idea what game the Arch is playing. All I know is he isn't backing down, so neither can I. I have to figure it out and stop him before I end up taking the fall for a crime I didn't commit.

My dad hasn't said a word to me all day. He's probably waiting for a verdict from Mr. Mayer before he drops the real punishment. When he jumps the gun on discipline, he has to deal with my mom. It's safer for him to make sure I'm really in trouble before he tucks a napkin into his collar and starts to feast on my backside.

At around three o'clock he leaves me alone at the shop to go run an errand. He can take all day, for all I care. I'm just tired of being watched like a prisoner.

I press my ear against the back door and listen for his car door to slam, then for his bumper to scrape as he pulls out of the alley. When I hear the sound of metal on pavement, I let out a deep breath. I'm finally alone.

I don't get to enjoy my Fortress of Solitude for long, and I jump when the phone rings. The ringer is amplified so we can hear it over the machinery when the shop is running. With all the machines silent, it sounds like a fire alarm. I ignore it until it goes to voice mail. Whoever's calling tries two more times before I've finally had enough of the noise and pick it up.

"Hello?"

The voice is familiar but I can't place it. "Chub? Open the back door."

My scalp flushes when I realize where I've heard the voice before. It's not filtered through an electronic scrambler, but it's the same voice I heard during the riot.

I try to sound menacing, even though I'm shaking. "Who is this?"

"Julius . . . Sizzler." There's a heavy knock on the door. "C'mon, open up."

"What do you want?"

"I've got *it*," he whispers.

"Got what?"

"My membership thing."

It dawns on me that I told him he needed to prove he wasn't still with the Arch. He must've come through.

"What is it?"

"Umm . . . you kind of hafta see it."

"Hang on." I tap the phone on my hand and consider my options. It's pretty simple. Trust him and open the door, or tell him to get lost. The way things are going, I need all the help I can get, even if it means taking a little risk.

"Okay," I say, and hang up the phone.

It's sunny, and my eyes have a hard time adjusting when I open the door. "It was you on the phone."

"No duh."

"Not now, at the assembly. You were the voice on the phone."

He chuckles. "Oh, yeah. Sorry about that." He twirls his cell phone. "That was, you know, before."

I scan the alley to make sure he wasn't followed. "Right." I wave him in, then close the heavy door and lock the dead bolt.

He looks around, grimacing. "Nice place."

It isn't.

His eyes rest on what's left of the Pile. "What's that?"

"That's my punishment for the fire in the locker room."

He winces. "Yeah, I heard about that. Archer's telling everyone you went crazy."

I guess that shouldn't surprise me, but it still makes me really mad. I step forward into the shaft of light coming through the back room's only window so Sizzler can see my eyes.

"Do I look crazy to you?"

He takes a step back. "Uhhhhh."

Suddenly I feel totally alone serving my unfair punishment. I need Sizzler to believe me. "I didn't do it."

"If I thought you did, I wouldn't be here."

For a minute neither of us speaks. He reaches into his pocket and pulls out a plastic sandwich bag stuffed full of something—presumably his initiation dues. I reach for it, but he pulls it back.

"You sure you want this?" he says.

"What is it?"

Slowly he hands over the bag. I hold it up to the light but can't tell what I'm looking at. I peel open the

Ziploc seal, and Sizzler quickly takes a step back, like I just opened a box full of scorpions. He looks like he might barf when I reach in and pull out the contents. Then I realize what I'm holding.

In my hand is a pair of underwear so badly skid-marked, it looks like it's been used to clean up a pelican after an oil spill. Had I pulled this out of the Pile, I would've thrown it straight in the trash.

I twirl the stained chunk of fabric in the air between us. "Is this a joke?"

He leans back to avoid the swinging mess. "No! It's what you wanted."

"I don't remember asking you to steal a pair of Skivvies from a crime scene."

"Read the label."

I reluctantly touch the little biohazard with my other hand just enough to straighten out the waist-band and see the label. To my surprise, Sizzler has come through after all. There is no way I can question his loyalty after this. Sewn to the band is a small white label, which reads: PROPERTY OF ARCHER NORRIS.

Jackpot.

I remember now. Archer's mom used to sew name tags into all his clothes after his coat was stolen on the playground. I try and fail to suppress a grin, and Sizzler relaxes.

"So?" he says.

"This is pretty good. You must really want in." I lower the underwear back into the bag and zip it shut. "Is there anything else?"

"Well . . ."

I tuck the bag into my pocket and fold my arms.

"Okay. There's one more thing." He pulls out his phone again and fiddles on the screen for a minute. When he finds what he's looking for, he shows it to me.

It's a picture of a sleeping Archer cuddling a plush doll and wearing the most severe piece of orthodontic headgear I've ever seen. The room looks pretty much the same as it did the last time I was in there years ago, except now trophies and sports memorabilia clutter shelves that once held comic books and action figures. He still has the same Harry Potter sheets I gave him for his birthday in first grade and the stuffed Wolverine I gave him for his birthday right before we started second grade. I didn't pick it, my mom did—don't judge me.

"I'll e-mail you the picture if you want it," Sizzler says, shaking me out of my fog.

Uncle Stosh always said, "Better to have and not need than to need and not have." I'm pretty sure he was referring to having picking fingernails long enough to scrape your brain, but it seems like pretty good advice in general.

"A couple of us stayed at his house Friday night. That's when I took the picture and got the . . ." He shudders a little. "I'm just glad to have them out of my pocket. What's your e-mail?"

The only e-mail account I have access to is Mrs. Belfry's. So I give it to him. "Ibelfry@alanmoore.edu."

He gives me an odd look as he types it in, hits send, and then pockets the phone.

"So, am I in?" he asks. The truth is he's come through bigger than I could've hoped, but I don't want him getting too big of a head about it.

"Are you sure this is what you want? I don't know

anybody who's ever chosen to be unpopular."

Sizzler thinks it over. "I never really thought much about any of this stuff before. I figured Archer treats you the way he does because he's cool and you're not—no offense."

I wave off the comment.

"I guess I had to get beaten at the only thing I've ever been good at to realize that cool isn't always what it looks like. There's always somebody cooler, or faster, or whatever."

"I saw the tryouts."

Sizzler shrugs. "Everyone did. He beat me in my best event."

"By a lot."

Sizzler hasn't been picked on and whispered about in the halls for years like the rest of us, but he still has a pretty good reason to take down the Arch. As the Colonel says, "My enemy's enemy is my friend," and I can definitely use a friend like him.

I make a show out of deliberating before extending my hand.

"Welcome to the cadre."

He hesitates and stares at my hand. I get nervous for a second, then remember what I was holding a moment before.

He makes a fist. "Let's do this instead."

"Okay, better idea," I say, bumping knuckles with him.

As I lead him to the back door, the possibilities that the underwear offers whip around in my mind like cows in a twister. If I play things right, I might even be able to use it to make the Arch confess to starting the fire.

I'm about to send Sizzler off when something else occurs to me. "One more thing," I say as I unlock the door. "Can I use your phone to look at a website?"

After a shot of Purell he hands me his phone, and I quickly search "poker Mace." The first result is a blog for a local poker league. I click on it. I can't risk my dad catching me slacking, so I just skim the home page.

Last night's post headline reads, *The Mayor impeached by Mr. X, Mr. X taken out by the Mace again*. I scroll down to a picture of my principal wearing a horrible white fedora. One hand holds a fan of cards over his face, the other is on a pile of poker chips. Next to him is a guy in a cowboy hat with a blue ostrich feather stuck in the front of the band like a hood ornament. The brim of the ridiculous hat casts a shadow over his face that covers everything his rug of a mustache and his sunglasses don't. I remember Mr. Mayer describing this guy in the stairwell. This has to be Mr. X.

I hand the phone back. It looks like Mr. Mayer's luck isn't improving any.

I stick my head out first to make sure the alley is clear, then hustle Sizzler out the door. My dad will be back soon and I still have some Pile left, but the work goes much quicker knowing what I know now. I have some excellent dirt on the Arch and Mr. Mayer, and my network of associates is growing stronger by the day. As much as I don't want to admit it, it looks like I really do have a cadre after all.

I sort the rest of the donated clothes at record speed but leave two items on purpose (an old blazer that smells like used cat litter and a gigantic bra I really don't want to touch) so my dad can witness me "finishing" my task right when he gets back.

A minute later I hear the telltale scrape of his bumper. I'm actually feeling pretty good, but when I open the door and let him in, I do my best to look like the weary, high-character kid he expects to find. I think he buys my act, because I swear he looks a little bit sorry for me as I make a show out of picking up the bra and tossing it in the trash.

CHAPTER 13

Normally, the McQueens look happy to see me, but this Monday morning all three of them look concerned. The head McQueen tips the hat at me. "Thought you were down for the count, boyo. What with the fire and all."

"I still might be. Mr. Mayer's in his office waiting for me right now." I'm actually surprised the McQueens are even willing to meet with me after the fire. It's the kind of thing people get kicked out of school for. It could generate the wrong kind of attention for anyone caught associating with me. They deserve some reassurance for their loyalty. "I didn't set the fire."

The one in the hat winks. "And I don't remember any of us asking if you did."

I'm not sure how to respond. "Guys—"

He interrupts, "As far as we're concerned, there's no further discussion required. Now, I believe you said something on the phone about dealing with the Arch?"

"It has to be done before Mr. Mayer suspends me. Otherwise, no deal." I give him my most serious look. "Can you pull off what we talked about last night?"

"Oh, we can do it," he says. "Question is, do we want to?"

I don't have any other options at this point. I can try to barter, but if they walk away, I'm toast.

"What's it going to cost?"

He glances over his shoulder at one of his brothers. "One of us, I'm not gonna say which, didn't do so hot on last week's history test. Doesn't reflect well on the three of us."

I see where he's going. "I've never changed a

grade before. This is new territory." It will be the McQueens' most expensive job yet but worth every penny if it works.

"Can you do it?"

I sigh loudly. "I think so."

He looks back over each shoulder at his brothers, then slaps a hand on my arm. "We have faith in you." The other two nod in agreement.

I'm glad *they* do. I, on the other hand, am sure I've bitten off more than I can chew.

I run through the plan in my mind one last time to make sure I'm not forgetting anything. "Are you guys sure you can handle him? He's not going to go along with this willingly."

"There are three of us. I think we can handle one kid, even an oversize one."

I reach into my bag and take out the item Sizzler gave me the day before. The hat reluctantly accepts the plastic bag and quickly hands it to one of the others. The one he gives it to wrinkles his nose and does a *Why me?* shrug.

"Because the Magna Carta wasn't Caesar's

go-cart!" the hat says. That answers whose grade I would be fixing.

"Remember, it has to be done before he decides to suspend me."

"Fair enough." He tips the cap at me, and the other two nod. "See you in detention." He winks as the three of them turn and go.

I walk to the principal's office as slowly as I can. The more time the triplets have to work, the better. Plus, I'm in no hurry to face Mr. Mayer. I'm not sure if it's school stuff or his troubles with this Mace character and his underground poker game causing his hair to turn gray, but I feel sorry for him either way, since neither one is my fault.

Mrs. Osborne shakes her head in disappointment when I walk in. I go straight to my usual waiting spot and plop down. A few seconds later Mr. Mayer opens the door, looking like he's aged about twenty years over the weekend. The headline I read on Sizzler's phone pops into my head. Mr. Mayer had another rough weekend at the poker tables. According to the blog, Mr. X and Mace were taking all the fun out of his secret hobby. I didn't have to read the whole story to know how bad a loss it must've been; it's written all over his face.

In his office he takes his seat, and I take mine. I look past him through the window to the courtyard outside. I have a clear line of sight to the second-floor walkway. If the McQueens are as good as I hope they are, they'll be out on the walkway any minute, and they won't be alone.

Mr. Mayer presses his hands in front of his mouth like he's praying to the patron saint of middle school principals, or maybe he's praying to the one for crappy poker players. He taps his index fingers nervously and studies me with bloodshot eyes. I touch my fingertips together and try my best not to look concerned. *What is taking the McQueens so long?*

After a minute he speaks. "Arson is serious."

I nod. "I know, but Archer Norris started the fire, not me. I was in the wrong place at the wrong time."

He rubs his forehead hard enough to remove skin. "I'm not kidding. This is one I can't just let slide."

I need to stall. "What makes you think I did it?" I say.

He laughs as though I just asked the most ridiculous question ever. "The student body president and captain of the track team was the only other person there. What would you think if you were me, given your track record?"

He has a point. It looks pretty obvious what happened. After all my hard work making sure I never got in trouble for my pranks, the reputation I've built myself is about to get me convicted of something I didn't even do.

On the elevated walkway that overlooks the courtyard, the door from the new wing springs open. *The McQueens to the rescue!* I sit a little higher in the seat, only to shrink back down when Carson Biggs and Tawny Phillips appear instead. Their eyes are glued to their phones. Carson and Tawny are the first kids in our school to admit they are "going out," which apparently means texting each other all day even though they are never more than two feet apart.

Mr. Mayer drones on. "According to school district policy, blah . . . blah . . . blah . . ."

But I'm not listening. The McQueens have to come through or I'm a goner.

"Blah . . . blah . . . suspension . . ."

"Huh?" I pull my eyes away from the window and look at him.

"Oh, did I get your attention?"

I'm about to say something, anything to stall for time, when the walkway door opens again. This time it's just like I planned.

Mr. Mayer doesn't notice my reaction and goes right on with his lecture.

A hatless McQueen comes through the door first, followed by the Arch, then the one in the hat. The bareheaded one stands with his back to the door so no one else can walk in on what's going on.

The phone on Mr. Mayer's desk beeps and he picks it up. "Yes . . . but the district doesn't need the TPS reports until Monday." He gives me the *One minute* sign and then goes back to explaining why the reports aren't done yet. I'm too wrapped up in the scene outside to listen to his conversation.

The hatted one stops the Arch in the middle of the

walkway and puts an arm around his shoulder. The Arch looks at his arm like a seagull just pooped on him, but he doesn't do anything about it. They both look over the railing to the courtyard below. When the McQueen gives a signal, the third triplet appears in the yard and walks straight to the flagpole. He's holding the bag containing the Arch's badly stained, undeniably personalized underwear.

The Arch's cocky grin fades as Darwin (?) calmly explains how things are going to go. When the one by the flagpole has his rubber gloves on, he reaches into the bag and takes out the awful garment, holding it up so the Arch can see it in all its skid-marked glory.

That's when the Arch goes mental.

It takes both McQueens to stop him from charging off the walkway. Mr. Mayer keeps blabbering and rubbing his forehead, completely unaware of the scene behind him. I resist a grin. Clearly, the underwear is the right approach. The Arch's reaction is better than I could've hoped. I glance at the clock on the wall. *Any time now.*

Delvin (?) clips the Skivvies to the flagpole's rope and attaches a paper banner with the words ALL HAIL THE NORRISTOCRACY below it. The first bell will ring soon. That's when everyone reluctantly walks through the entrance to Alanmoore to start another week of drudgery. The courtyard will be crammed with kids rushing to homeroom, and they will all see the official flag of their new student body president. My only hope is that he cares so much about his reputation, he'll do exactly what the McQueens are . . . requesting.

I jump when the first bell sounds. The triplets must be a lot stronger than they look, because he tries to get away, but they hold him back. The Arch just watches, a defiant look on his face, as the third McQueen begins hoisting the undies up the flagpole. Time stands still. He needs to make up his mind before anyone sees his underpoos flapping in the breeze, or the story will spread faster than lice.

Maybe it's already too late. Carson and Tawny walk back the same way they came a minute before, and the Arch stops struggling as the two lovebirds smirk and tap away at their phones. I grip the arms of my chair, half hoping they'll see the underwear and text a picture of them to everyone they know. The Arch eyes them nervously as they pass, oblivious to the underwear, and they get to the door without ever once looking up.

Mr. Mayer hangs up the phone and is looking at me like he expects me to say something.

My future will be decided in the next few seconds. My scalp gets hot.

Mr. Mayer throws his hands up in frustration. "Well?"

I look back outside and read the hatted one's lips as he leans in close to the Arch's ear: "Well?"

This is the moment of truth.

"Maciek, were you even listening to me?"

Outside, the doors leading into the courtyard start to open. The Arch must hear this, because his eyes get wide, then he nods hard like he's trying to shake spiders out of his hair. The hat signals to the one by the flagpole, who quickly lowers the battered banner and tears it off the line just in time. The two McQueens lead the Arch back inside, weaving their way through the herd of kids trying to get to homeroom before the bell rings.

"If you aren't going to say anything, I don't see that I have any other choice." Mr. Mayer removes a very official-looking binder from his desk drawer and pulls out an even more official-looking form.

"Mr. Mayer?" I stall. I should just tell him I suspect the Arch is up to something bigger than the pranks during his speech and hope he believes me. "The truth is . . ." I stall with a dramatic sigh, stretching the moment as long as I can.

I've played the only hand I can. It has to work.

There's a gentle knock on the door. I release my death grip on the chair and take a deep breath.

"Come in." Mr. Mayer puts down his pen.

Mrs. Osborne sticks her head around the door. "Mr. Mayer? There's another student here, Archer Norris. He says he has some new information about the fire."

I smile but then quickly go back to my serious face.

Mr. Mayer's shoulders drop and he shoots me a look. I shrug.

"Bring him in."

The Arch's face is beet red. I don't think he likes the position I've put him in.

I stand up. "You two probably want to talk alone."

"Sit down, Maciek," Mr. Mayer says. "You too, Archer."

The Arch takes the seat next to me and stares at his toes. I fight the urge to look over at him. I don't want him to look up and see how sweaty my head is right now.

"Do you have something to say, Archer?"

The Arch mumbles something and Mr. Mayer shifts in his seat.

"This is a very serious incident, and I have two students with different versions of what happened. Suspensions are my only option until I find out the truth." He looks back and forth between us. "Look, I don't know what the deal is with you guys, but it has to stop before someone gets hurt."

I chance a look at the Arch. He chews on one of his fingernails like he used to when he got nervous. I need him to tell the story the McQueens told him to tell.

"It's okay, Archer. Tell him what happened."

His lip curls like he caught a whiff of a fart. He rolls his neck once and says, "The fire wasn't Chub—I mean Maciek's fault."

Sizzler is right. The Arch is willing to do almost anything to hold on to his office and his reputation. It makes him vulnerable, but it also makes him unpredictable until I figure out why it means so much to him.

"I had to cut the string on the waistband of my track uniform. Maciek was helping me burn the ends so it wouldn't fray, the way Coach Farkas taught us to do to our shoelaces."

Mr. Mayer looks at me, expecting me to add something.

"Shoelaces." I nod, not wanting to interrupt the Arch's story. He threw in the bit about Coach Farkas on his own; it's a nice touch.

"The lighter got hot, and I dropped it in the cart and it just . . . burned."

Mr. Mayer lets out a deep sigh. He looks from me to the Arch and back. "So it was an accident?"

"Yup," we say.

He considers it for a moment, then puts the form back in the folder.

"There will have to be detention."

"Of course," I agree.

The Arch just grumbles.

Detention I can handle. Plus, it will give me the chance to get Sizzler's embarrassing picture of Archer off Mrs. Belfry's e-mail.

The bell rings to start the school day.

"Shouldn't you boys be getting to homeroom?"

We spring to our feet and scurry out before he changes his mind. A weight is lifted off my chest, and I can't wait to get the cadre together to start figuring out what the Arch is really up to.

In the hall he turns to go to his homeroom, in the other direction.

"Pleasure doing business with you," I say as he walks away.

He stops in his tracks, then slowly turns and walks back toward me. The top of my head isn't even up to his chin. The graceful, gravity-defying spikes of his overgelled hair taunt me—a constant reminder of what he has and I don't, thanks to him. But when he gets close, I see past the cool hair and grown-up-looking face. His eyes remind me of the look Mr. Mayer has. *Desperation?*

He leans in close, and the cloud of Axe body spray makes it hard to breathe. "Savor the flavor, *Chub.* This isn't over. It's only the beginning."

CHAPTER 14

Mr. Funk's face is buried in his newspaper, so he doesn't see me sneak into homeroom after the bell. I'm bursting at the seams to tell Moby about the untidy-whities plot the McQueens and I just pulled off, but he and Shelby don't even look my way. I can't tell if they are upset or just playing it cool.

Word of the fire has obviously spread, and I get more than the normal amount of dirty looks from some members of the track team.

As Mr. Mayer reads the announcements, someone behind me whispers, "Nice of you to make it, Matchstick—uh—I mean Ma-chek."

Six or seven kids chuckle, but I doubt their collective IQ is over a hundred, so I ignore it.

After homeroom I go to the lockers, but Moby isn't there. There's only one place he can be.

I check under the doors of all five stalls, but there are no feet. This is officially the longest I've gone without talking to Moby since second grade.

I cut through the library and take the secret stairwell to avoid running into Archer or any other angry members of the track team. I want to feel good about the way things worked out this morning, but the look on the Arch's face and his parting words have me shaken up. Now that we're engaged in open warfare, one of us will win and one will lose. For the loser there will be no way to keep his defeat a secret.

Moby isn't in the cafeteria at lunch. The McQueens are sitting at a table, but it's probably best we aren't seen together for a while, so I go talk to Shelby instead.

"Have you seen Moby?"

"As a matter of fact, I have." She's more awkward and moody than normal.

Why does every conversation with her have to be like pulling my teeth out? "Where is he?"

"I don't know. He disappeared before I had the chance to talk to him. Should we be talking in public?"

"Sure," I say. "Why?"

She leans in and whispers, "Isn't the cadre in trouble over the uniform fire? You know—*rule five*?"

"What the heck is rule five?"

She looks puzzled. "I assumed he disappeared because of rule five. If we're ever in trouble . . ."

I suddenly remember making up the thing about rule five, but I can't wipe the confused look off my face fast enough.

Shelby deflates a little and her bird gaze softens. "There is no rule five, is there?"

"Shelby . . . ," I say, not even sure how I'm going to finish the sentence. But I don't have to finish it, because she pulls her own version of Moby's disappearing act. Only hers isn't as good, since she's taller than everyone else in the lunchroom and her flamingo stride is hard to miss.

I almost go after her, but I don't want to cause even

more of a scene. I'll apologize for the rule-five thing next time I see her.

As the day wears on, I get the picture. Moby is avoiding me.

After school I go to the spot behind the Dumpsters where we usually meet to walk home. He isn't there. I scan the street and catch a glimpse of his enormous backpack disappearing behind the building next door. I want to chase him down and ask him if I did something to tick him off, but I have to report to detention and I'm already late.

Detention lasts an hour, but the drama club meets on Mondays for two hours. After I serve my detention, I'll finally go to one of the meetings and hopefully Shelby will have calmed down a little. I've seen flyers trying to recruit actors for the new play. Maybe if I talk to her about that, I can get her to forgive me, so at least one of my friends will be talking to me.

Mrs. Belfry puts her hands on her hips and gives me the kindest, most disappointed look ever. "You just can't stay away, can you?"

She has to pretend to be upset that I got in trouble,

but I think she likes having some company after school. Not to mention my Laptop 101 classes.

I shrug as she turns and waddles off to her office.

I follow her because I need to get on her computer and pay some "bills." She goes to sit in her chair as I say, "How's the refraction on your keratometer? Are the levels normal?"

She stops before her butt hits the seat and stands back up. She clutches her sweater closed and shoots the machine a suspicious look. "I'm not sure. How would I know?"

"Oh, you'd know."

"Would you look at it for me?" Her voice has a hint of desperation.

It's so easy I *almost* feel bad.

Almost.

First thing I do once I'm logged in is pay off my debt to the McQueens and do a little bit of routine maintenance on my own record. Then I check the Arch's grades. They're good—a little *too* good. Why would someone as smart as he is choose to act like a brain-dead caveman? I make a few changes to his grades here and there, but not enough that anyone might notice. Just enough so that it will add up by the end of the year.

Next I go into Mrs. Belfry's e-mail and print the picture of the Arch asleep, drooling all over his headgear. I'm not sure if I'll ever use it or not, but better to have a copy on me in case I ever get in a pinch. I pull it off the printer and stuff it into my pack. Looking at it, I get a twinge of sadness. At first I think it's because of all the fun I used to have at his house, but then I decide it's because of Wolverine. Archer and I always argued over who was better, Batman or Wolverine. I like Batman because he's just a normal guy who got dealt a crappy hand and does what he needs to do to make it right. It figures Archer would prefer the mutant with special powers. Batman has issues; Wolverine has an indestructible Adamantium skeleton. Cry me a river.

After business is done, I bring up the blog for Mace's poker league. Mr. Mayer's losing streak is worse than I thought, which explains all the new gray hair. There's post after post about Mr. X taking Mr. Mayer down, only to lose in the final round to Mace. The thought of having to give away money you've earned because someone flipped over the wrong card makes my stomach hurt. No wonder Mr. Mayer is aging so fast.

Mrs. Belfry sticks her head around the corner as I'm closing everything down. "Is it working properly?"

"It is now." I stand and head toward the door. "Good thing I was here today."

She clasps her hands together and sighs.

"I'll check on it again tomorrow, just to be sure," I say.

"Such a nice boy," she says as I walk out of her office.

I head to the fire extinguisher case and fish around behind it for something to read. I pull out a copy of *Scott Pilgrim* I've read a million times before and flip through it to pass the last half hour of detention. I don't actually read it; I'm too distracted wondering what's up with Moby. He's disappeared on pretty much everyone at one time or another, but he's never done it on me before and I don't like it. I'm starting to understand why Shelby was so upset when we rule-fived her.

Three thirty feels like midnight when it finally arrives. I wait an extra ten minutes after my official release to give the Arch time to leave the school after his detention. The last thing I need is to run into him face-to-face. I wave good-bye to Mrs. Belfry and head down the stairs to find Shelby and the drama club.

There's a note taped to the door in Mr. Mayer's writing: "Drama club canceled."

That's weird; it must've been a last-minute cancellation. Shelby would've said something about it if she'd known earlier. So much for that plan.

My parents will be at the shop for another couple of hours, so I take a detour on the way home. I've never been to Shelby's house, but I know which one it is. I walk up the path and ring the bell, scanning the street. I can't be too careful.

When the door opens, I'm looking through a portal into the future. Shelby Larkin is standing in the doorway, but her hair is gray, her face is wrinkled, and although I would've thought it impossible, her glasses are even thicker.

"Yes?" says old Shelby. She leans down to inspect me and pushes her glasses up just like normal Shelby does. Everything about her is familiar, including the sweater she wears over her shoulders like a cape. I'm pretty sure normal Shelby wore the exact same one to school last week. I don't want to offend this person, or cause a tear in the space-time continuum, but there's business to attend to. "Is your . . . is Shelby here?"

"Who would like to know?" She has the same *I'm smarter than you* tone as Shelby.

I look around, not sure why she's asking that, since I'm the only one here. I guess weird runs in the family. "Me, Chub."

She wrinkles her nose at me, then turns and calls for Shelby.

Old Shelby and I share an uncomfortable silence waiting for the real Shelby to come to the door.

"Thanks, Grammie," Shelby says when she comes down the stairs.

The old lady walks off and Shelby waves me in.

"I thought that was your mom," I say.

"My mom . . . doesn't live here. It's just me and Grammie."

"Oh." I don't know what to say. "That's cool."

Shelby stares at her feet. She must still be upset about the rule-five thing. I think back to the morning after the Shanghai sucker punch assembly and how mad she got at us for ditching her. I need to tell someone about what happened this morning, but I need to apologize first.

"So," I casually say. "I'm sorry."

She folds her noodly arms and looks up from her toes. "Excuse me?"

Saying it once was hard enough, and now I have to say it again? I take a breath and look her in the eyes. "I said, I'm sorry."

"Sorry for what, exactly?" She taps her foot.

Seriously? "For ditching you and making up rule five, okay?" If she doesn't accept that, I'm gonna have to find someone else to brag to.

"And you won't ditch me again?"

I suppose that's reasonable, now that the cadre is actually a thing. I nod.

"Then I accept your apology," she says.

She leads me into a side room that's more like an antique store than someone's house. There's stuff everywhere, and I have to search for a place to sit. I pick up a mountain of mail that's on the couch so I can sit down. Every single unopened letter is addressed to Shelby in loopy handwriting like my mom's. One word pops out from the return address as she snatches the envelopes from me: "Penitentiary."

Shelby's mom is in jail? I suddenly feel bad for having two parents at home that I try to avoid.

She looks at me and it's obvious she knows I saw the return address.

"Where's your dad?" I say, hoping to avoid the subject of her mom.

She rolls her eyes. "He died before I was born."

This is not going well. It's probably better if I just let her tell me what she wants me to know instead of me asking any more stupid questions.

"I never knew him." She points to a table covered in framed photos. "Just through pictures." The biggest picture is of a young guy with his arm around a Shelby look-alike that has to be her mom. "It was me, Mom, and Grammie until Mom went away."

I don't want to make Shelby relive any more bad stuff, but the curiosity is like an itch in the middle of my back. Is Shelby's mom some kind of psychopath? It would explain a lot. I have to know. "What did she do?"

Shelby takes a deep breath. "She stole a bunch of money from a guy she worked for."

"Why did she steal money?"

Shelby throws her hands up. "How should I know? I guess she thought she needed it more than he did."

I'm starting to think the hardest part of being an adult is holding on to whatever you've earned. "Then what?"

"Then she got in trouble and she left. It's been me and Grammie ever since."

As far as I can tell, she doesn't have any friends other than Moby and me, and the only other person she hangs out with is probably older than Mrs. Belfry. Now it makes sense why Shelby always acts and dresses like she's sixty.

She crams the letters behind the couch and neither of us speaks.

"Ask your friend if he would like something to drink," Grammie Larkin calls from the other room.

I nod, and Shelby calls back, "Yes please, Grammie."

Every time I move, dust puffs out from the couch, threatening to make me sneeze. It looks like it's irritating Shelby's eyes too. For once they aren't staring into my soul like she wants to suck my brain out. In fact, she doesn't look at me at all. There's something else bothering her.

When it's obvious she isn't going to start a conversation, I ask, "Why no drama club today?"

"It's canceled, Maciek." She pulls a cloth handkerchief out of the sleeve of her sweater and wipes her eyes and nose.

I see an actual tear, and my guts turn to Jell-O. Plotting the overthrow of a student body president or blackmailing my principal is one thing, but dealing with a crying girl scares the heck out of me.

"Well, I guess I'll have to wait until Wednesday to meet the rest of the club, then," I say, hoping to make her feel better.

Apparently, it's the wrong thing to say, because the tears really start to gush.

Grammie Larkin comes in carrying a silver tray with a small plate of cookies and a tea set on it. She pours out two tiny cups of steaming tea and then leaves the room without ever noticing Shelby's tears. After dealing with having a daughter in jail, a few tears probably didn't even show up on her radar. Say what you want about my parents, but you can't say they don't notice me. Now it makes sense why Shelby is always trying to hang out with us. I think about how much time I've spent trying to avoid her for no reason, and I feel a little sick. People have disliked me for no reason since second grade. I should know better than to treat someone that way.

I pick up one of the cookies from the tray and take a bite as I wait for Shelby to come around. The cookie tastes like butter and dust, but I try to act as if I like it so she won't cry anymore.

Finally she stops and looks up at me, her eyes bleary behind her glasses. "The Kangaroos," she says. "The uniforms."

"Huh?"

"The track team needs new uniforms because the old ones got burned."

She isn't into sports; why does she care about the track uniforms?

"So?"

"So, the new student government met at lunchtime today to figure out how to buy them."

"Okay."

"The track team is the pride of the school, and uniforms aren't cheap. There's only so much money in the budget for student activities. Archer Norris proposed a motion to take the money from the extracurricular clubs and use it to buy the new uniforms."

"He can't just do that, can he?" It sounds so wrong.

"The class elected him to be the 'voice to the faculty.'" She quotes Mr. Mayer at the assembly, only with a snarky tone. "The vote on the clubs was three to one. Sherman Mills voted with Archer and Troy. It's all over. There is no more drama club, Maciek."

My hand clenches into a fist, crushing the cookie back into dust. I may not have actually ever gone to a meeting, but that club is the most important thing to Shelby. It means as much to her as track does to Sizzler. Probably about as much as my only friend meant to me in second grade. Why should everyone else have to pay for the things he destroys? Plotting against me is one thing, but Shelby never did anything to him (that he knows of). The Arch is making a path of destruction through the school and he doesn't even *care*.

This is exactly the kind of thing I feared when I heard about that stupid election. Archer Norris got a little bit of power and now he's using it to trample whoever he wants just because he can.

Something inside me snaps. The Arch has messed with a member of the wrong cadre for the last time.

Now it's going to cost him.

CHAPTER 15

By the time I get to Moby's, my mind is a hurricane with everything we need to discuss. The Colonel pulls open the door and waves me inside.

"Is Moby here?" I ask. But then I spot his backpack by the bottom of the stairs.

The Colonel makes a *psssht*. "He's upstairs, turning his brains into mush." This is adult code for playing video games, but "mush" is an exaggeration. Moby could barely even *soften* his brain with the lame games his parents allow him to play. "Go on up."

"Thank you, sir."

I'm almost to the stairs when the Colonel says, "I

figured you'd be up there with him right after school."

I can't tell the Colonel I was in detention and have him think I'm becoming a dirty hippie, but I don't want to lie to him either, so I split the difference. "I was . . . working in the library today."

He raises his chin and looks me up and down. "Doing a little civil service, eh?"

"Yes, sir," I say, then turn to make my exit.

"Well, the library's not the military, but it's a start," he says.

I nod, then wait a second to make sure there's nothing else. I'm about to head upstairs when he says, "I ever tell you boys about my buddy Lenny? Talk about a civil servant."

Normally, I love to hear the Colonel talk about almost anything, but I have some major stuff to discuss with Moby, and I need to get out of here quickly so I'm home before my parents. The sooner they find out that I'm not in trouble for the whole arson misunderstanding, the sooner I can get out from under the microscope and get down to some serious scheming. I've got to bring Archer down, and I've got to do it soon.

I try not to sound impatient. "Nuh-uh."

"Lenny and I joined the army and went to boot camp together. We used to stay up late and play hearts every night after lights-out. Good times."

"Hearts?"

He shoots me a look. "It's a card game. Back then video games were called cards. That's how we passed the time. Anyhow, after basic training we ended up in the same unit. All told, we fought in two wars together." He sighs. "That will bring a couple of friends pretty close."

I don't know where he's going with this, but I hope he gets there quickly. "He sounds like he's a really good friend."

"*Was*," he says. "Lenny died in—well, it's classified. But I'll just tell you this: Lenny sacrificed himself to save me without even thinking twice. If I'd seen that grenade first"—he takes a deep breath—"I would've done the same for him. You see where I'm going with this?"

For a guy who's so in love with the army, he sure doesn't make it sound very appealing. "I think so."

I didn't realize he knew how to smile, but he does. "If you're going to *have* that kind of friend, you need to make sure you *are* that kind of friend."

I nod the way my parents like to see me nod when they are trying to teach me a valuable lesson. It has the right effect on the Colonel, because he smiles again, then says, "That is all." Then he turns and marches off to the kitchen, leaving me alone in the foyer.

The Colonel usually knows what *he's* talking about, even if he doesn't always know what *we're* talking about, so before I head upstairs, I stop and think about what he said. Moby has always been that kind of friend, but have I?

Moby is sitting on the floor in the theater room, staring up at the screen. His brain might be a little mushy, judging by the drool running down his lip. He twitches when he notices me, but his eyes stay locked on the game. On the screen a cartoony turtle floats around on a cloud sprinkling sparkle dust on some grumpy mushrooms, turning them into sunflowers. I think this game is designed for five-year-olds. I stand by the wall just inside the door and wait for him to notice me.

After a few minutes I can't take any more of my best friend ignoring me, and I clear my throat loudly.

"I know you're there," Moby says. "I saw you walk in."

"Did you see me looking for you at school today too?"

He doesn't turn to look at me. "Why were you looking for me?"

"To tell you some good news."

"What? Did you get some more people to join your cadre?" He gives me a look I've never seen on his face before.

It looks an awful lot like disappointment, and I feel really bad.

"Moby, why have you been avoiding me all day?"

He keeps sprinkling stupid sparkle dust.

I step between him and the screen. "Hello!"

Moby pauses the game but won't look me in the eye. I know him; I can tell he's trying to figure out a way to escape, like he always does when things get uncomfortable. The fact that we're at his house is probably the only reason he doesn't make a break for it.

"It's almost time for *Extreme Bunker Builders.* I'm going to have to let the Colonel use the TV," Moby says.

"Well, then I guess you better hurry up and tell me why you don't want to talk to me."

"If I tell you, then I'll be talking to you, and that will sorta ruin it."

The kid has a point, but I'm not going to back down.

"C'mon, Mobe, you've been my friend forever. We're like Green Hornet and Kato."

He finally looks at me. "Why are we friends, Chub?"

The question hits me like a punch in the stomach. "Because we are. I don't know." I'm starting to wonder if cornering him and making him talk was such a good idea.

"Well," he says, "I know why I'm friends with you. Back in second grade I used to get so nervous at school because I didn't have any friends, and I just wanted to hide all the time so no one would see me. The day we met, I was in the cafeteria and my stomach was all upset from stress, and because my parents had made falafel and tahini the night before. I had to blow off a little gas blast so I wouldn't poop my pants, so I waited for it to get real loud in there, then I tried to let out a quiet little fart to let off some of the pressure."

I remember that day like it was yesterday. It was the day we became friends. A grin creeps onto my face as I remember what happened next.

"The fart started out silent, but then the whole place went completely quiet for a half a second. I was so nervous everyone could smell it already—I just let it go." Moby hangs his head.

"The fart heard round the school," I say, remembering the giant blast that introduced me to my best friend. "How could I ever forget that?"

"I wish everyone would." Moby closes his eyes like the memory is a bad smell he's trying to avoid. "After it happened, everyone was laughing at me . . . almost everyone." Moby looks up at me, but I can't meet his eyes. "That's why I'm friends with you. You didn't laugh."

I wanted to be his friend because of the exact same fart. Because he looked straight at me that day, with the cloud still hanging in the air, and then walked away like it was no big deal. It was one of the coolest things I've ever seen. Funny how two people can see the same thing so differently.

I want to say something, but he's finally talking to me again, so I don't interrupt.

"We were the only two people who didn't laugh. It's been you and me ever since, until last week."

It's true—since our group has gotten bigger, he and I have had less time together. "Are you mad about the cadre?" I ask.

"The Green Hornet is a hero no matter what. The only reason anybody cares about Kato is because the Green Hornet needs his help."

I honestly thought having more people to help would make things easier, but it never occurred to me Moby wouldn't see it that way. I became so focused on my enemy, I forgot about my best friend.

"You're upset I got Sizzler to steal the Arch's underwear instead of you?"

He shoots me a look. "What?"

Then it dawns on me that he doesn't even know about the whole Skivvies scam.

"Listen, Mobe. I needed to blackmail the Arch so he'd say the fire was an accident. Sizzler had a pair of his messy underwear, and I—"

He shakes his head. "You never would've blackmailed the Arch without me before."

He's right. I wouldn't have. But things are different now. The Arch is much more dangerous, and I need to fight him any way I can.

But when I look at Moby's face, something hits me I never thought of before. Everyone else is in the cadre because of the Arch. But Moby is here because of me. He's stuck by me since the beginning, and lately I haven't been a very good friend in return. I need to make sure Moby has a key role in all our activities. The trick will be figuring out a key role he can't mess up with one of his improvisations.

"So let me get this straight. From now on you want to be the only one who gets to handle other people's dirty underwear?" I try to hold a straight face, but I crack, and then Moby laughs too. Laughing with him makes me feel like everything is good in the world, at least for a little while.

"Something like that."

"You know the cadre needs you, right?" I shove him in the shoulder.

Moby cracks a small grin and shoves me back. "Yeah."

That's the thing about best friends—you don't have to say everything to know what the other guy means. I grab the extra controller off the shelf and get down on the floor next to him. I have half an hour before I need to leave, so we activate two-player mode and start turning mushrooms into sunflowers together. I need some gaming time with my best friend. Back when it was just Moby and me, it seemed like we goofed around a lot more. Lately, going after the Arch has started to feel kinda like work. Managing people can really wear you out.

"You know the Arch is up to something major?" I say.

"Yeah, I heard about the drama club. That sucks."

"If somebody's up to something, you follow the money."

We didn't know the Colonel was there, and his voice makes us jump.

"This isn't a government operation, Grandpa," Moby says. "It's just some stuff at school." Moby rolls his eyes at me.

"Well, take it or leave it, that's my two cents," he says, taking a long drink out of a glass of watered-down soda.

"We need to figure out what the Arch is up to." The picture I got from Sizzler pops into my mind. It's the only play I have at the moment. If the Colonel isn't going to be of any use, maybe I—we—can use the photo somehow to get the Arch to reveal himself.

The Colonel releases a belch like the roar of distant cannons. "Pack up the fairy dust, boys. Time for my show."

CHAPTER 16

Jarek doesn't work on Mondays, so he comes over to our house for dinner later that night. He gets there at the same time as my parents, which is great because he makes a nice buffer between my dad's jaws and my butt. I avoid my parents until dinner is ready by pulling a Moby-style bathroom session to think about the best way to use the photo of the Arch. My legs are numb when my mom calls us all to the table. As I walk downstairs, I pray my dad is in a good mood. How his day went could make or break a delicate operation like this.

After Dad says the blessing, it's quiet as we all dish

up. I'm about to speak up when my dad says, "There was no call from the school today." He glances at my mom. "I will call the principal tomorrow."

This is it.

I say the line I've rehearsed: "We explained what happened to Mr. Mayer. I'm not in any trouble." I know it won't end the conversation, but it's a solid start.

My dad looks at me and then at my mom. "What did you explain?"

"We were trying to melt the end of the drawstring on his uniform, and it got out of hand."

Dad gives me a suspicious look. "Why were you doing this?"

I swallow a huge chunk of fried potato. "The little plastic thing came off the end of it, and it was fraying—"

"Aglet," Jarek says through a mouthful of brussels sprouts.

My mother snaps her fingers at him because she doesn't allow talking with food in your mouth. "Jarek! What would Nastusia say?" Nastusia is Jarek's mom, my aunt back in Poland. I don't remember her, but her name is brought up only during the enforcement of rules, so she's probably pretty scary.

He forces the sprout down. "Sorry, Aunt Zofia. The little plastic things on the drawstring are called aglets."

There's more silence. My dad is probably trying to comprehend why someone would know this piece of information. Then he shakes his head at the "youth of today" and says, "Why are you lighting *anything* on fire at school?"

I'm prepared for this. "Well, it was a perfectly good drawstring—except for the missing aglet—and Archer and I didn't want our parents to have to spend money on a new set, so we took the initiative."

Jarek laughs but disguises it as a cough.

"Why didn't you tell us this right away?" My mom looks at me over the top of her glasses.

This is going better than I could've hoped. There's an old Polish saying about this: "The man is the head of the household, but the woman is the neck." Dad won't tear me up if Mom doesn't let him, and it looks like she's buying it.

I have to tread lightly for the next part. I put on my

best weary-child-laborer look. "Dad never really gave me the chance to explain. We went straight from school to the shop, and then I was on the Pile all weekend."

My mom shoots my dad the look that we all know means they will be discussing his lack of patience after I'm in bed.

Dad wisely avoids eye contact with her. Instead he turns to me and says, "You should hang around with people who are a better influence."

"Let's just be happy nobody got hurt." Mom puts the subject to rest.

I push a slice of kielbasa around my plate with my fork like it's a little hockey puck, while my parents and cousin chow down. I can't stop wondering what the Arch might be up to. Did he burn the uniforms just so he would have an excuse to take away money from the clubs? Framing me would be the cherry on top, but I can't see the point of going through all that just to mess with a few unpopular kids who prefer chess and drama to running in circles around the football field.

After dinner Jarek and I clean up the kitchen.

"Your dad's been talking to my dad." A vision of me sweating away in a potato field flashes in my head. It's not what I want to hear.

"What are they talking about?" I try not to sound concerned.

Jarek stops drying a plate. "You know what they're talking about, Mr. Potato Head." He grabs a raw potato off the counter and pretends like he's picking it off a branch.

"Potatoes grow underground," I correct him.

"Don't remind me. I've spent years forgetting all about these nasty things. Listen, I left there with thirty dollars in my pocket for a reason."

"Because you always wanted to work in a movie theater for less money than most kids get for an allowance?"

He shakes his head. "Make jokes, but it's still better than digging these out of the ground all day. Did you know that my father has a tractor that will do the work automatically, but he loves to make kids pick them by hand anyway?"

I nod. I know this because he's told me about two

thousand times. “Whatever you are doing that’s got your dad talking to my dad, my advice is to knock it off. They think you are soft because you aren’t being raised in the old country. All they need is a good excuse to send you over for a little toughening up.” He tosses the perfectly good spud in the trash can across the room. It hits the bottom with a thump, and he throws his arms in the air and yells, “Gooooooooaaalll!”

“It’s not that simple.”

“Maciek, I’m older than you. I’ve learned a lot in those extra eleven years, and I know one thing for sure. You don’t want to choose to become a potato farmer. Trust me, you just don’t.”

Later Jarek helps me with my homework in between discussing which new movies are coming to the Clairemont and speculating about the plot of *League of Honor*. I tell myself not to get too fired up for it, since given the way things are going, I will probably be in a different part of world when it comes out.

“Do movies open the same day in Europe as they do here?” I ask.

"Just got the first X-Men movie three years ago." He doesn't even blink as he crushes my hopes.

My dad knocks once, then opens the door to my room. "I have an appointment tomorrow afternoon. Can you work for me at the shop?" he asks Jarek.

"Sorry, I'm getting a shipment of popcorn tomorrow," Jarek says.

My dad grumbles. I can tell he doesn't completely buy the excuse, but it doesn't faze him. "Maciek, please come to the shop after school."

I start to protest, but Jarek mouths the word "potato" at me behind Dad's back, so I just nod instead.

The next morning Moby and I meet at the corner a few blocks from school, where we usually meet. We wait for Shelby to join us instead of making her chase us down like usual. She has her arms in her sweater like a normal person for once, so she looks only forty years old instead of sixty. Moby is quieter than usual even before Shelby shows up, but he doesn't try to disappear, which I take as a positive sign. We all agree the first thing we need to do is talk to the other members of the student government and figure out how the Arch got them to shut down the drama club so quickly. There's no point approaching Troy Gilder, since he's basically the Arch's puppet. That leaves Sam Hardwick and Sherman Mills.

"I'll talk to Sam," Shelby offers. "Since she's a girl too."

I'm about to crush the joke she's just served up for me, but Moby beats me to it. "As far as we know," he says.

I almost give myself whiplash turning to look at my friend. Did Moby just make a joke in front of another person?

Moby and I decide to talk to Sherman together, since he's the treasurer. He's the one who actually moves the money around, so he'll know where the club money is going. We catch up with Sizzler before the first bell. We need his help to corner Sherman long enough to talk.

At lunchtime Moby and I wait behind the Dumpsters for Sizzler to show up with Sherman. I'm relieved our guest arrives under his own power. The Arch dragged me to the meeting in the locker room against my will, so it feels like a method to avoid. When Sherman sees Moby and me, his eyes go wide.

"Wait, you're . . ." Sherman looks at Sizzler and then at Moby and me. "You're on the track team! What are you doing with these two losers?"

"We got us a cadre now." Sizzler folds his arms over his chest. "And Archer isn't who you think he is."

Sherman narrows his eyes. "Really? Cuz I think he's the fastest kid in school now and Coach Farkas knows it. I think you want these two to help you take him down so you can have your spot back."

"Fair enough, but that don't mean he isn't up to some bad stuff," Sizzler says.

"Sizzler's with us now," I tell Sherman. After all, we called the meeting, not him.

I can practically hear the gears turning in Sherman's head as he does the math on his chances of escape. He runs a hand through his middle school version of a comb-over and says, "I shouldn't be seen with you."

"Why not?" I say. "Maybe I voted for you."

"Because *I'm* in student government, and an honor student, and *you* tried to burn down the school."

Sizzler shakes his head.

I wave my hand, letting him know I've got this. "Is that what the Arch told you so you'd vote to shift the club money to buy new uniforms?"

"It makes sense, doesn't it?" Sherman shoots back. "You started the fire. Why should the track team suffer?"

It does make sense in a weird way. It probably wasn't a difficult sell for the Arch. He called the student government together and got them to vote on how to spend the money before word got around that I didn't start the fire.

I step close to Sherman. "So how do we undo this?"

He laughs. "Only the president can call a vote. Maybe you should pay more attention to how these things work and less attention to being such a spaz all the time. What do you care about the clubs, anyway? Are you the defender of the weak and nerdy or something?"

He's trying to get me to lose my cool, but I'm not going to. "So what happens next? How does the clubs' money end up as new uniforms?"

"No idea. I've only been the treasurer for, like, five days," he says.

Sizzler folds his arms over his barrel chest. "We can wait."

A bead of sweat appears on Sherman's temple. "Archer's dad got us a discount on some new uniforms, so he's handling all the details after I get him the money."

"The money that's supposed to go to the clubs," Sizzler adds.

"That"—Sherman's eyes narrow—"is up to the student government."

It's all a little too simple. A week or two ago I would've thought it was a pretty big coincidence that the Arch was already lining up a deal on new uniforms, but with what I've learned about him lately, I have to assume he's somehow planned all of this. "When does he get the money?"

"He's bringing the receipt for the uniforms to our

meeting Monday. As soon as I have it, I can give him a check."

I touch my fingertips together and glance at Moby. Without my meaning to, a grin spreads across my lips as I remember the Colonel's words from the day before: "Follow the money." Maybe the old guy isn't losing it after all.

We let Sherman go with the promise that we will be talking again soon, and he scurries past Sizzler like he's sneaking around a chained pit bull.

Moby asks, "So, what's the plan?"

"We do what you're always supposed to do in cases like this." I pause to let him fill in the blank. Moby just shrugs. I don't think he listens to the Colonel as closely as I do. "We follow the money."

I report for duty at the shop after school, the whole time cursing my cousin and wondering how difficult it can possibly be to receive a shipment of popcorn. For the next couple of hours I press shirts, put them on hangers, bag them, and arrange them on the carousel in alphabetical order. Without my dad here, the mood in the shop is a lot less slave labor–ish. My mom actually asks me how it's going every once in a while and even compliments my work occasionally.

Before I know it, she's turning off the lights and flipping the sign in the front window from OPEN to CLOSED. As she counts out the day's deposits, I empty all the trash cans into one big bag and head to the back door.

I pull open the door and my heart starts racing. A huge, dark shape fills the doorway, and it has a hand raised above its head, ready to swing at me. Instinctively I jump back and toss the bag of garbage at the would-be robber.

"Chub!" says a familiar voice.

I relax out of my standing armadillo pose. "Sizzler?"

Sizzler kicks garbage off his sneakers and dusts off his pants. "What the heck did you do that for?"

"I thought you were trying to rob me," I say before I realize how lame it sounds.

"Supposably there's a pretty big market for stolen garbage. Looks like I hit the jackpot." He laughs.

"Very funny. And it's 'suppos-*ed*-ly.'"

He looks at me like I just sprouted a second head, and then he shakes his.

If I'm gone too long, my mom will come looking for me, and I don't feel like having any more discussions about another new friend and what kind of influence he is. "I assume you didn't come over here to make jokes?"

"So, I went to that spot behind the Dumpsters after practice to avoid Archer until my mom came to pick me up."

"And?"

"I heard someone whispering, sounded like they were on a phone call."

He has my attention.

"They were against the wall, by the parking lot. I stuck my head in the space between the Dumpsters to hear. It was the Arch."

My scalp tingles. Secret phone calls are always good. "What did he say?"

"Well, since I only heard his side of the call, it didn't make a lot of sense, but he sounded desperate. He kept saying he needed to get a fake ID."

Fake ID? I've seen enough movies to know that kids need fake IDs to do things they aren't supposed to do. Why in the world would Archer need one?

"Did you hear anything else?" I say.

He's about to answer when my mom hollers from the front, "*Rodzynek?*"

Sizzler's forehead wrinkles. "Is that Polish? What's it mean?"

Polish parents call their kids *rodzynek* for some reason. It means "raisin," but there's no way I'm telling him that.

"Coming," I call back, ignoring his question.

Sizzler shakes his head. "Did I do good?"

"No, Sizzler. You did not do *good*," I say, shaking my head at him.

He looks stung.

"You did *well*."

CHAPTER 17

I skip to the front of the store, practically shaking with excitement at the possibility of figuring out Archer's secret and paying him back for years of humiliation once and for all.

When I'm not working at the shop as a form of punishment, my mom lets me pick something out of the lost and found as pay. Once, after working all day on a Saturday, I got an old wool trench coat that almost brushed the ground when I put it on. I wore it when I was Voldemort for Halloween last year. My dad showed me how to clean it up and make it look and smell almost brand-new. I think it might be a women's coat, but nobody at school has noticed that yet, so it's cool. The coat is the best thing I've ever gotten from the lost and found, but there are a few other items in there I'm hoping nobody will claim. It's the only cool thing about working at the shop.

My mother smiles at me, holding out the box that serves as our lost and found.

"Decide what you want for pay, Maciek."

I flip open the box and scan the familiar contents for anything new. Something wedged flat against the side of the box catches my eye, and I pry it loose. It's a playing card, a king with a red heart in the corner.

"What is that?" She looks over the top of her glasses.

I show her the card and she scowls like it offends her. "Why do you want that?"

The card shows a king with a blank expression, oblivious to the fact that he's sporting the worst neck beard ever, not to mention that he looks like he's stabbing himself in the head with his own sword. I grin and slide the card into my pocket.

"There's a nice beanbag in there," she says, like she works at a used beanbag lot and needs to sell me one.

"I want the card," I assure her.

She shakes her head, unable to understand where she went wrong raising a child who'd rather have a worthless playing card than a perfectly good denim pouch filled with dry legumes.

Work is over and I need to get the cadre together to decide what to do with the info from the phone call Sizzler overheard. But first I have to talk to the one guy who'll know why someone would need a fake ID. Hopefully, he'll have an idea about what our next move should be. I have to get to Moby's house to see the Colonel.

I make a big show of stretching and rubbing my neck like my dad does when he gets home after a hard day at the shop. My mother gets the appropriate look of concern. "What's wrong, *rodzynek*?"

"I'm just so worn out from working today. I forgot, me and Moby have a project for school we need to work on." I try to look as pitiful as possible.

Parents may know how to use guilt, but kids know how to use sympathy.

She considers it for a second, checks her watch, then says, "I'll drive you."

My mom waits in the driveway for the Dicks to let me in. It takes longer than usual for someone to answer the door, which means the Colonel himself must be coming. When the lock turns from the other side, I wave at my mom.

The Colonel yanks the door open and scans the neighborhood. After a moment he looks down and notices me.

"Chub." He nods.

"Colonel."

He's wearing socks with little suspenders around his calves holding them up, boxer shorts, and a T-shirt that says, I'M ROOTING FOR THE JAPANESE.

He scans the street one more time. "What are you waiting for, draft papers? Get in here."

"Where's Moby?"

He taps an imaginary watch on his wrist. "It's seventeen twenty. Where do you think he is?"

If you know Moby, you know that five to five thirty is one of his regular bathroom times and you better just get used to it.

"I forgot. I can wait. By the way, nice shirt," I say. "But didn't we fight Japan in World War Two?"

He gives me a weird look. "You bet your sweet—you bet we did. Why?"

I point at his shirt.

His chins form a turtleneck of skin as he looks down. "Oh, this is for *Whale Wars*. They took their whupping like men in WW Two. No point holding a grudge once you beat an enemy."

What's he talking about? That ruins the whole point of kicking someone's butt in the first place.

"Got *Whale Wars* paused in the other room." The Colonel jerks his thumb toward the TV room.

"Mind if I watch it with you?"

"You aren't gonna cry, are you?"

I straighten up. "Not unless the dirty hippies win, sir."

"All right," he says, turning and heading off toward the theater room. "Might be a bit of a wait, anyway. I've been sneaking Moby cheese when his parents aren't looking. This could take a while."

Later, as the closing credits of the show come on-screen, Moby appears. He's a little winded, but no more so than usual.

"Hey, Chub." He wipes his forehead with his sleeve. "What's up?"

I can't hide my smile. "We need to talk."

When I'm done telling him about my conversation with Sizzler, he looks at me blankly.

"What do you think it means?"

The Colonel mutes the TV and shifts around in his chair. "Fake ID, huh?"

I nod. This is precisely what I hoped would happen. If anyone knows why someone would want a fake ID, it's the Colonel.

"Who is this kid?" the Colonel asks Moby.

"He's a kid in our class," Moby says.

"He a friend of yours?"

"No, he's our nemesis."

"Uh-huh," the Colonel says.

"We know he's up to something," I say. "Why would someone want a fake ID?"

He kicks back in the chair, extending the footrest, and laces his fingers behind his head. He's in his reminiscing pose; we're about to get something good. "When I was sixteen, I lied about my age to join the army. Maybe this kid's a patriot, wants to join up and give back to the country that—"

"I don't think that's what it's for, Grandpa," Moby says.

The Colonel snorts. "Well, that's a shame." He puts his arms on the armrests and drums his fingers. "Probably using it for no good, then."

"Like what?" I ask.

He gets a faraway look in his eyes as he considers the question. "Anything you can't do unless you're an adult, I guess," he says. "Why, with a fake ID a guy could do almost anything. . . ." He proceeds to list just about every activity my father says is wrong with the world today. But the difference is that when the Colonel lists them off, he talks about them like they are all his favorite flavors of ice cream. "Buying cigarettes, getting alcohol, gambling—"

That grabs my attention. “Wait, you need ID to gamble?”

I think hard. If the Arch had been smoking or drinking alcohol, I’d have smelled it or someone would have talked.

The Colonel rubs his boot brush of a haircut. “You need ID unless you have as much gray hair as me.”

Could gambling be the secret the Arch is so desperate to keep? Did he lose all his allowance playing cards somehow? The Arch is supercompetitive, so it makes sense in a weird way. But should someone who’s willing to throw perfectly good money down the drain like that be allowed to handle the money for the new uniforms?

I reach into my pocket and touch the king of hearts. “Thank you, sir!”

“Glad I could help.”

“Moby, we have some calls to make.”

He springs into action, grabbing the phone off the end table.

“You boys going to get that kid in trouble?” the

Colonel asks as we scurry out of the room.

"We're not sure what he's up to, sir. But we're going to find out," I say.

The Colonel ponders it for a moment. "Fair enough. Just remember, he's still a kid like you boys."

I stop in my tracks. Sometimes I forget the Arch and I are only a month apart in age. Being in trouble for kid stuff is one thing. I'm starting to think he's gotten himself into some kind of adult trouble.

"And remember one other thing too."

"What's that, sir?" I turn around.

"You tell that boy, no matter how bad he screws up"—he straightens up and puffs out his chest—"there's always a place for him in the US Army."

I'll have to remember to tell the Arch that—right after I crush his empire of lies.

CHAPTER 18

The next morning I wake up late and have to hurry to meet the cadre and the McQueens before school. We need to plan our next move. The stress of running a cadre is really affecting my sleep. At least I don't have any hair to lose over it.

There's a lot of chatter when I tell Shelby and the McQueens what Sizzler overheard last night. I call the meeting to order.

"We know our beloved student body president is hiding something. I think what Sizzler heard is the key to figuring out what it is."

The spokestriplet gives me a knowing look. "Why do I think you have an idea what it might be?"

"I'm not sure, but I have a hunch," I say. I still can't understand why Archer would blow his allowance on a lame game, but it's the only thing that makes sense after hearing the Colonel's list of reasons for a fake ID. "We'll only get one chance to nail him, so we'll need proof."

"Tell us what it is, and we'll help you get your proof." The other two McQueens nod like both of their heads are attached to the same string.

It's the perfect chance for me to make it up to Moby for hurting his feelings during the flagpole plot. "This one stays between me and Moby until we have absolute proof." Moby stands a little taller. "You guys are going to have to trust me."

One by one everyone in the circle nods.

"So, what do you want us to do?" Shelby folds her arms, annoyed at not being let in on the secret.

"I'm so glad you asked," I say, grinning. "Because I happen to have a plan. Sizzler, are you still close to the Arch?"

"Don't know," Sizzler says. "He hasn't said a word to me since our little talk with Sherman the other day."

"But you're still on the track team, right?" I say.

"Yeah."

"Which means you can keep an eye on him while Moby and I do what we need to do?"

Sizzler bobs his huge head. "I can watch him."

"Good. I hope you're all free after school today. Here's what we're going to do. . . ."

There's the normal amount of talk about me at school that day. In the halls I hear the same whispers I've been hearing for years—"lice," "bald," "spaz"—but now there's a new one as I walk by an open classroom door on a bathroom pass. Someone inside the classroom calls out, "Firebug," which gets a laugh before the teacher tells them to cool it.

The cadre eats lunch together, all of us trying to keep the excitement about our after-school mission under control.

The hatted McQueen shoves a handful of Tater

Tots into his mouth. When they're mashed to a slobbery pulp, he says, "Oh! We heard a new one about you today, Chub."

Kids are always starting rumors about me. I'm an easy target.

"Is it the one about me being adopted from the circus?" I say.

All three McQueens laugh, and Shelby gives me a pitying look.

"No," says the hat. "But I do like that one. Word on the street is that your parents' business is a front."

"Huh?"

"Yeah, word is the real business is laundering money for the mafia. Pretty good, right?"

"What does that mean?" Shelby asks.

"My grandpa and I saw it in a gangster movie once. Laundering money is where you take stolen money and run it through a business or something legal so the cops can't trace it back to a crime," Moby says. "Mafia guys do it all the time."

It seems like there's a new surprise from Moby every day.

"My parents *have* laundered money," I say, to a bunch of gasps.

"The Russos own that Italian restaurant a block away from our shop. They dropped their entire deposit into a drum of olive oil one night, and the bank wouldn't take it. My parents used the big machine to clean it for them."

Everyone sits back in their chairs, bored by the real story. The truth is never as good as the legend.

When the final bell rings, the entire cadre meets behind the Dumpsters to go over the plan once more before getting to work. The only one who isn't there is Sizzler, who can't be late for track practice and risk the wrath of Coach Farkas.

We leave school together, heading to the Arch's house to snoop around for proof he's up to what I suspect.

"Are you sure this is a good idea?" Shelby asks. "Breaking and entering is a crime."

"First of all, we aren't breaking anything. The latch on Archer's window has been broken since first grade."

"So?" she says, missing the point.

"So, you can't break something that's already broken."

Moby connects the dots. "So we aren't breaking . . . we're just . . . entering."

"Exactly," I say. "And just plain *entering* isn't a crime. Besides, if all of us stick to our part of the plan, nothing can go wrong."

Shelby will be our lookout in case the Arch somehow slips away and Sizzler can't warn us in time. The McQueens will distract Mr. and Mrs. Norris, and Moby and I will sneak into the Arch's room. He won't risk keeping anything incriminating at school. It will be in his room.

The Arch's house is a few blocks past mine, but when we were friends, I went there so much I could've ridden my bike there with my eyes closed. It's far enough out that the businesses and sidewalks are replaced by woods and fancy signs telling you the name of the neighborhood you are entering. If I lived here, I'd save every penny I had to make sure I never had to move into a neighborhood like mine.

I know all the good hiding spots within three blocks of the place. I position Shelby at the school bus stop half a block away because it has a clear view both up and down the street, as well as a direct line of sight to the Arch's bedroom. She'll give the signal if the Arch somehow evades Sizzler and comes home early, or if the McQueens' distraction doesn't work. Moby will see it from the Arch's bedroom window, and we'll have plenty of time to escape before we get caught.

It's always some little thing that gets you caught. I read that after all the stuff Al Capone did, they sent him to jail for messing up his taxes. The lesson is, don't take silly chances, especially when you are doing something not quite legal. We can't risk being spotted by someone out walking a dog or something, so Moby and I decide to approach the Norrises' house through their backyard rather than from the front. We creep out of the bushes and hide behind an ivy-covered shed that used to be my best spot when Archer and I played hide-and-seek. I sneak to the corner of the shed, where I can easily see the big tree in the Norrises' front yard.

The McQueens show up right on time. They stroll up the street and a moment later set up to execute their diversion. One of the hatless triplets flops down on the grass under the gigantic maple tree, his brother kneeling next to him. The one in the hat gives them the thumbs-up, then marches to the front door and rings the bell.

A moment passes before I hear the door open.

"Hello, can I help you?" I can't see her from where I am, but I would recognize Mrs. Norris's voice anywhere.

"Good afternoon, miss. I'd like to talk to you and your husband if I could." The McQueen takes off his hat and wrings it in his hands.

"What's this about?" she says.

"Well, miss, it's about that very inviting, very dangerous climbing tree you've got in your front yard."

Two of the triplets are on the lawn, one acting injured and the other pretending to try to help him.

"Is that boy okay?" Mrs. Norris sounds very concerned.

"That's what I'd like to talk to you and your husband about."

"CHARLES!" she yells. "A boy fell out of the tree in the yard. You better come see."

"Not again!" Mr. Norris's voice booms from inside.

When Mr. Norris appears on the front porch, Darby, I think, starts rolling on the ground, moaning and holding his stomach. His brother pats him on the shoulder to comfort him, a concerned look on his face.

"Good afternoon, sir. My name is Darwin McQueen, and that unfortunate boy is my brother Darby," the spokes-McQueen says.

Both Norrises rush out onto the lawn to help the fake faller, and I glance toward the bus stop. Shelby waits a few seconds to make sure the McQueens have set the hook and then signals the all clear. We cautiously step out of the secret spot behind the wall of ivy and sprint to the window on the side of the house. I pray they haven't fixed the latch since last time Archer and I sneaked in. When I press on the frame, it squeaks slightly as it slides up, and I let out a breath of relief that no breaking was needed. All we have to do is enter. A minute later we are in.

I haven't been in Archer's room since second grade, and not much has changed. As I noticed in the photo that Sizzler took, the one difference is all the trophies wedged onto shelves that used to be full of books and action figures.

"Keep an eye on Shelby," I tell Moby. "If she gives the signal, you tell me and we go."

"Got it."

He takes up his post by the window, and I start my search. I'm not sure what I'm looking for exactly. The bed is unmade, the silly old Wolverine doll lying on the pillow. The headgear the Arch was drooling all over in the picture sits on the bedside table, looking like something you would use to catch a bear.

I start with the most obvious place you'd hide something, under the mattress. Next I check under the bed, and then behind the bookcase and in the closet, the whole time listening for the single ring of the Norrises' home phone. That's Sizzler's signal that Arch has left track practice early.

"How's it going, Mobe?"

"Just watch, man." He doesn't turn around.

For once he's sticking to the plan, so I go back to searching. Something in Sizzler's photo caught my eye before, so I pull it out of my pocket to look at it again. I walk to the other side of the bed, where Sizzler must've stood when he snapped the picture. I look at the picture, then at the shelf in the background. For some reason it looks different in the shot than it does now that I'm standing here. Behind me, Moby lets out a sigh. I turn around and he's still watching out the window. *I guess I'm watching the watchman.*

I look at the photo and then the room. The picture was taken from a different angle because Sizzler is over a head taller than me. What can't I see from my height? My eyes flick back and forth from the image to the actual room, checking off each item that appears identical. But as I work my way to the top of the bookcase, something in the photo stands out. It's on the top shelf, blocked from my view. I tuck the picture away and climb up on the bed.

I stretch to reach the thing and drag it off the shelf. My scalp flushes as I realize what I have in my hands. I've only seen it in bad pictures from a cheesy blog, but there's no mistaking the big, goofy cowboy hat with the blue ostrich feather in the band.

Gotcha!

The visit to the Colonel has paid off. Finally I know what the Arch has been hiding. As I suspected, he's been using the fake ID to gamble. He is as tall as the average adult, at least an inch or two taller than Mr. Mayer. When he puts on the hat, covers his face with sunglasses and a fake mustache, and doesn't talk very much, there's no reason he can't pass for an adult. Of course, the hat solves only half the mystery. What does all of it have to do with his presidency and the uniforms? Now that I know what he's been hiding, it's only a matter of time before I figure out the rest. I smile, imagining the look on his face when I tell him that I've uncovered his secret.

"I got you, Archer," I whisper under my breath. My hands ball into fists, crushing the brim of the hat. "Or should I say, Mr. X?"

"Evil genius!" Moby says, shaking me out of my self-congratulatory trance.

I whip around, but he's still watching the window. I climb gently off the bed.

"No . . . way," Moby says.

"Oh, yes way!" I reply. I look outside, expecting to

see Shelby calmly manning her post. Instead she looks like a flamingo trying to take off with its feet nailed to the ground.

The signal! I nearly drop the hat.

I stick my head out the window just in time to see all three McQueens sprinting away in the opposite direction, one of them holding his hat down on his head as he runs.

Moby doesn't budge.

"Moby! I thought you were the . . ."

I look down. In his lap is a tattered copy of *Watchmen*.

"Archer has *Watchmen* too," he says, as though it's somehow good news.

I slap my head. Shelby is running up the street now, her arms and legs like four propellers in her awkward flamingo stride. The front door slams and Mr. Norris yells something about "no-good con men."

"We gotta go!" I whisper, shoving Moby toward the window. He tries to keep reading, but I shove him as hard as I can and say, "NOW!" Finally he drops the comic and starts to move.

There's only one thing to do with the cowboy hat—I put it on my head and dive out the window, shutting it quickly as Mr. Norris's footsteps thud down the hall.

Moby is ahead of me as we sprint for the woods. Mr. X's hat bobbles on my head, and I don't even try to keep the smile off my face as we run like crazy.

CHAPTER 19

We all rally at my house after the mission. I show the cadre the hat I took from the Arch's room and bring them up to speed. The cowboy hat is all the proof I need that Archer is actually the mysterious Mr. X from Mr. Mayer's poker league. A kid pretending to be an adult so he can play poker has to be illegal. But why mess with the clubs at school? Why mess with me? Is he afraid I'll find out and expose him, or is there more to it than that?

I need to confront the Arch about the hat, and I need to do it somewhere he doesn't have an advantage. School is his turf for now, so I'll check the schedule on the blog and confront him at the bowling alley next time Mace's poker league meets. I'll give him the chance to apologize for betraying me and to give the money back to the clubs. If he refuses, I'll use what I know to take him down.

Sizzler uses his phone to check the poker blog. The next event is the last one of the year, the semifinal qualifier for the regional tournament this Friday night at Thunder Alley Bowling and Fine Dining. Archer can't afford to make a scene there or everyone will realize Mr. X is just a kid.

Sizzler reads off his phone, "'The top five finishers are automatically in the regional tournament, where the prize is ten thousand dollars.' No wonder Archer is so nervous. That's a lot of money."

The thought of getting that much money for winning a game of cards makes me dizzy. I think about all the things my parents could do with $10,000.

"So what's the plan?" Sizzler asks. "Beat him at his own game?"

Everyone looks at me.

"I don't know how to play poker."

"But think about it," Shelby says. "The poetic justice of you swooping in and taking his victory away from him!"

I have to admit, it does sound pretty good. I better figure out how poker works so I can come up with a plan to beat the Arch. If he can win against adults, including our principal, it can't be all that tough. Can it?

"Sizzler, can I use your phone for an hour or two to learn how poker works?" I ask.

He hangs his head. "Too close to using all my data this month with all the other stuff I've done for the cadre. My parents will kill me if I go over again."

I think for a minute before the obvious solution comes to me: Mrs. Belfry's laptop. But my excitement dies when I realize that won't work. Mr. Mayer knows me too well. If I suddenly start volunteering in the library after school, he'll know something is up. It won't take long for Mrs. Belfry to tell him how "helpful" I am with the computer, and then I'll be in real trouble. If I want to get on her laptop without raising any alarms, I need to play it just right.

I smile as the simple brilliance of my plan hits me. "Sounds like I'll be getting detention tomorrow."

The trick to getting detention on purpose is pulling off a stunt that walks the line between detention and suspension. After going through the prank supplies in my locker, I decide to go with a good old-fashioned stink bomb, but I'll set it off in an outside passageway so it won't gas out the inside of the school. If any classes have to be canceled, there will definitely be a call home, followed by a one-way ticket to Potato Land. It's too much of a risk now that I'm so close to bringing Archer down.

I stand in the breezeway between the main school building and the gym and let off the bomb. Within seconds kids are running every which way to escape the rotten-egg stink. The sulfur cloud burns my eyes and makes it hard to see, but the shape of a person comes toward me. Moby walks right through the toxic cloud and stands next to me, just like I did once with him in his moment of need.

"What are you doing here?" I ask.

"You're trying to get detention without me."

"Yeah, and Mr. Mayer will be here any minute." I shoo him away.

But he refuses to go. When it's clear he isn't going to leave, I give up, and the two of us stand there waiting for the principal.

When he shows up a minute or two later, his eyes are ringed in red like he hasn't slept in a week. I may be wrong, but I think seeing me there, claiming credit for the prank, actually makes him a little relieved. None of us say a word as we make the long walk back to his office to do the paperwork.

Mrs. Belfry is happy to see me when I walk into the library to serve my sentence after school. She claps her hands in front of her mouth when she notices I also brought a friend with me.

Moby gives me a weird look as I explain to Mrs. Belfry that the Dalek virus is going around the Internet and that she better update her TARDIS drivers so her computer doesn't catch it. Because of all the "help" I've given her, she pulls out chairs for us and leaves us alone to do what we need to do.

We spend the entire hour searching everything we can find on how poker works. We hit the blog first. Looking at the pictures of Mr. X, I can't believe I never realized it was the Arch before. In almost all the pictures he's next to a scrawny guy in a leather jacket. The captions tell me that he's Mace. The only thing cheesier than the thick, fake-looking gold chain around the beanpole's neck is the grin on his pimply face. I was expecting a fat, old movie mobster; this guy barely looks old enough to shave.

Next we go on YouTube to watch some tutorials. It's confusing at first because nobody seems to be playing with real money, but pretty soon we figure out that you have to buy little plastic poker chips and bet with those instead to make it easier to count. The videos show us the different combinations of cards you can play and which ones give you the best chance of winning. They explain how to act like you have good cards when you actually don't and bad cards when they are actually good. I'm even more confused than I was when we started. I doubt I could even shuffle a deck of cards, let alone play well enough to take down a real player. I need to scrap any dreams I have of beating the Arch at his own game. I'll just have to work this thing out with him the way civilized people do—with blackmail.

If I'm going to sneak into the basement of the bowling alley and see the poker league in action, I need to blend in. A mustache worked for the Arch; now I need to get one of my own.

Before we leave school, we meet Shelby in the drama club room.

When I tell her we need a mustache and a wig, she gets a look on her face that's halfway between giddy and constipated.

"Are you okay?" I ask.

The look tips toward giddy and she claps her hands together. "I'm just savoring the irony."

"I see," I say, even though I don't.

"Archer shut down the drama club, and now we are going to use the props to exact our vengeance!" Her glee bubbles over like a soda poured into a glass too quickly.

I've never seen her get excited about anything before, let alone cackle, but it's pretty cool. Maybe I'm starting to rub off on her.

Shelby lugs out a wooden toolbox that's bigger than she is. She makes a big show of opening all the drawers and picking through their contents. When she closes the box, she shows us what she found—a wig, a fake mustache, and some glue. I'll use the disguise to sneak into the game and spy on Mace and Mr. Mayer, then confront the Arch with the hat so he can make his choice.

The three of us go to Moby's house to try out the disguise.

The Colonel is in a recliner in the living room taking a very loud openmouthed nap. It's good he's asleep, because we can't afford to have adults start asking questions when we are so close to taking down the Arch. Plus, his snore sounds like a herd of buffalo drowning in a tub of butter, which is good. If it stops, we'll have a minute or two of warning, so he won't walk in and surprise us at work.

"Hold still," Shelby says as she plasters glue on my

face. She uses way too much to get the mustache to stick and almost seals my mouth shut. I suspect this is not an accident. When I have the wig on, I check myself in the mirror and hope like heck that I appear old enough to get through the door.

I look like an adult, all right, one whose body suddenly shrank down to the size of an eleven-year-old. The effect is not convincing. Am I really going to sneak into an underground poker game looking like a grown-up who got left in the dryer too long?

As I'm pondering this, Moby reaches over and rips off the mustache.

"OOOWW!" I yell, and rub my face.

"Lemme try." He slaps it on his own lip. Next he takes the wig and puts it on.

I don't want to admit it, but like all my friends, Moby has gotten taller than me recently, and he makes a much more convincing adult than I do.

Shelby pushes her glasses up her nose and looks him up and down. "Sorry, Maciek," she says. "It looks like the role of Poker Spy One has just been cast."

The gears in my head grind, then start turning. "Moby," I say. "Does your dad have a suit that fits you?"

Friday morning I drop a note in the Arch's locker.

Thunder Alley: Tonight. Come get your hat back, Mr. X.

I don't sign it. I figure I don't need to.

That night my dad is out running some mystery errand, which makes it easier to get away. Jarek gets me out of the house by telling my mom he needs my help at the theater, and then he drives Moby and me over to the bowling alley. In the car I hand Moby the tube of glue he'll need to stick the mustache to his face. He needs to sneak into the game to make sure Mr. Mayer and Mace don't wander out and catch me and the Arch having our showdown.

We hustle through the lobby and walk downstairs to the basement together. I hang back while Moby goes to check in. The lady watching the door doesn't give him a second glance as he strolls by wearing a suit that's just a bit too big. Either the light is really bad or the lady doesn't care, because she waves Moby right through. So far, so good.

When he's barely inside the door, he looks back at me, smiles, and throws me a double thumbs-up. I shake my head back and forth to get him to put his thumbs down, but he just nods back, his smile all but hidden by the ridiculous mustache.

He disappears into the dark room, so I turn and climb the stairs to the lobby. There are plenty of witnesses around in case the Arch decides to pound me into dog food. We're early, so I kill some time feeding the claw machine a few quarters while I wait. A stuffed kangaroo toy slips through my grasp a few times before I sense someone behind me.

I turn around and he's there. With all these adults around he doesn't look as big and scary here as he does at school.

There's a long silence as we each wait for the other to talk.

When it's clear he doesn't know what to say, I go first. "You got my note?"

"Yep." He stuffs his hands in his pockets.

I'm not positive, but I swear it looks like he's about to cry. What does he have to cry about? Maybe he finally feels bad for everything he's done to me.

"So, why did you do it?" I say.

"Do what?"

"Let's not insult each other. I have all the pieces, I just don't know how they fit together yet." The guy at the counter looks over at us. I take a deep breath and lower my voice. "Why don't you start with why you burned the uniforms?"

He takes a deep breath and looks around. "You think you're so smart, but you don't have a clue."

"I don't, huh?" I spit. "You left some pretty big ones for me. Calling yourself Mr. X doesn't make you one of the X-*Men*, Archer."

He snorts.

I lower my voice more and take a step closer to him. "I know about Mace and the poker. I also know you've been losing. The only thing I can't figure out is what any of this has to do with the school. You might as well tell me. I'm going to figure it out eventually." My heart beats like a jackhammer.

"Or what—you're gonna blackmail me?" he sneers. "Go ahead. Mace won't care if I get in trouble with my parents or at school. How do you think I've kept playing even though I've been losing so badly? I owe him a ton of money, and he'll figure out a way to make me pay him no matter what. The only way out now is to win and pay him off. When I win, it'll be over."

I've seen enough movies to know what a real bad guy will do to you if you don't pay up when you owe him.

"Who is this Mace guy, anyway? He looks like the kind of kid you'd shove around at school."

"I'm surprised he isn't your hero," Archer says.

The comment catches me off guard. "What the heck does that mean?"

"He's a shady little jerk who likes to manipulate people, just like you."

Is that what he thinks? That he's some sort of good guy and I'm the problem? I can't let him throw me off track.

"Archer, you're a kid. You can't go back in there

and play anymore. Mr. Mayer's an adult, and look what it's doing to him."

His head dips. "I don't have a choice."

"There's always a choice."

"You think it's easy being the Arch?" He raises his head. I can't tell if he's angry or sad.

Try going bald in second grade and see how you like it. "Am I supposed to feel sorry for you because everyone thinks you're awesome? Give me a break."

"You're so dense. You act the way you act because it's what people expect from a lice-infested nerd. It's no different for me. People want the Arch, so that's who I have to be. You only think it's great because you don't know what it's like."

"Oh, is it tough being the student body president and everybody's hero?" I say.

He shakes his head. "Nothing at school is a challenge for me anymore. I don't even have to break a sweat and I can smoke everyone on the track team." He pauses and sucks in a deep breath, working up to what he's about to say. "At summer baseball camp I made it onto one of the teams with some high school kids.

They were cool, and after lights-out they taught me how to play poker. It was hard at first, but I was good at it. By the end of the first week I'd won all their money." He smiles a sad smile. "One of them introduced me to Mace later that summer and it just . . . got out of hand."

I take the edge off my voice. "So you're going to keep playing? You're just going to get yourself deeper in trouble?"

He uses the toe of his Converse to kick at a piece of gum stuck to the carpet. "Mace has these games rigged so he can win when he wants to, but he doesn't run the regional. I already in it. When I win, I can pay him off and be done once and for all."

"And if you don't win?"

He kicks the gum harder. "I have to at least try. I only need to come in second to pay him off. The only reason I can't beat him here is because he cheats. Second place in a fair game is a sure thing."

I run through it in my head. "But you're a kid. How will you even get into the regional?"

"Fake IDs are easy to get if you know the right guy. Mace is going to hook me up."

"Why would he want you in the tournament if you can beat *him*?"

"Me playing in this tournament is a win for him no matter what. If I win, I can pay him back. If I lose, I'll have to borrow more from him. Either way he gets paid."

I'm really starting to dislike this Mace.

There's still one thing that doesn't fit. "And how does all this help the school get new track uniforms?"

"My dad's company is donating them. I asked him last year when I heard about the whole student government thing if he'd donate them if I became president, and he didn't even blink. They get a tax break or something for the donation."

"You've been planning this since last year!"

He nods. "I figured if I was student body president, I could keep the donation a secret and frame you for the fire. The student government gets to decide how to spend the money the school makes on bake sales and stuff. If the uniforms were ruined and everyone blamed you, it wouldn't be tough for the student body president to redirect that money to buy new ones. All I had to do was get Sherman or Sam to vote for it. Once they did, I have Sherman write the check to Mace's fake company, then I show up with the uniforms and nobody knows the difference. But I guess you're not going to let that happen, so I have no choice but to play in that tournament."

Now *that's* a plot! I shake my head, more out of admiration than anything.

I reach behind the claw machine, where I stashed the cowboy hat. He holds out a hand for it, but I pull it back.

"You're right. I'm not going to let it happen. If you try to take that money, you will get caught. This has gone way too far," I say. Constantly plotting against the Arch is taking a toll on me. Now that I know how deep of a hole he's dug himself, I don't know if I have it in me to go in after him.

The harsh light from the game hits his face. His eyes have the same look they had in my basement the day he killed my hair, and our friendship along with it. "Is there anything else you want to say to me?"

He snatches the hat. "It's almost over."

Before I can say anything back, he turns and sprints out of Thunder Alley.

Is it possible the same forces that formed the Arch also formed me? That we are both just living out the expectations of a bunch of kids we don't even really know? I've spent the last few years trying to be the opposite of him in every way. But neither of us would be who we are without the other.

I've read enough comics to know a hero isn't a hero without a villain. The only question is, which one of us is which?

People drift into the lobby from the basement. The game must be winding down.

I better get Moby out of there before he improvises something and gets himself in trouble. I'm in a fog walking back down to the basement when the lady at the door stops me.

"I just need to get my . . . friend," I explain.

She folds her arms. "No interrupting the players while they're playing, kid. Why don't you go try the claw machine and win yourself a stuffed toy while the adults finish their game."

I suspect the claw machine is as rigged as Mace's poker league, but I keep that to myself. "Oh, he's not playing," I say. "He's the guy over there." I look into the gloom of the basement and try to make out individual shapes through the darkness and smoke.

When my eyes settle on Moby, I start to sweat.

He's not in the corner watching everyone else play. He's sitting at one of the tables, stroking his fake mustache, and holding a pair of cards just like the players we watched on the Internet.

But the thing that really makes me rub my eyes is the gigantic stack of chips on the table in front of him.

CHAPTER 20

When Moby finally gets up from the poker table, I've gnawed my nails down to nubs. A guy leads him off to a corner of the basement, where they disappear for a minute. As I wait for him to reappear, a deflated Mr. Mayer pulls on his jacket and skulks to the door. I quickly duck into a coat closet so he doesn't spot me, then watch him as he walks up the stairs shaking his head. So he didn't snap his losing streak tonight. I scan the faces of the other players as they file out. Most of them look tired, like Mr. Mayer has lately.

An eternity passes, and I decide Moby must've pulled one of his escapes and slipped out a side door.

When he finally appears, he looks like he's trying to race out of the room holding a pool ball between his butt cheeks.

The lady at the door doesn't pay him much more attention on the way out than she did when she waved him in. "Congratulations," she says flatly.

He hustles by her, then takes the stairs two at a time.

I catch up to him in the lobby and grab his sleeve. "Moby!"

He turns and looks at me, the fake mustache still stuck on his face. "Hey, Chub."

"What the heck happened in there?"

He throws a paranoid glance around, like the Colonel does when he answers the door. "I think we should go outside first."

I don't realize how musty it is inside Thunder Alley until the cool night air hits me. We find a shadowy spot away from the lights of the parking lot, and Moby hands me a heavy envelope. I open the flap and gasp.

It's stuffed with cash. I feel light-headed holding it, wondering if my parents have ever even touched that much money before. I gawk at Moby, then the cash, then back at Moby. He still looks confused.

"So, wait. You won?" I say.

"Not really. I came in second."

"But how did you have money to play?"

He looks around again. "I didn't. The lady who let me in told some guy that I was there. He gave me a bunch of chips to play with, but he didn't make me pay. When I left, he took the chips back and gave me this."

I run through it in my head. It doesn't make any sense. Who would just give some kid a bunch of money to play . . . of course! It's as plain as the 'stache on his face. Moby was lured into the same trap the Arch was. He accepted the chips thinking they were free, only to find out he owed money for them later. The difference is Moby won, so he didn't have to pay anything back.

"That's why the Arch is in trouble," I explain. "Mace lends him money, then cheats to win it back. Then Archer ends up owing Mace the original money he borrowed."

Moby shakes his head like a disappointed parent. "That does sound like something Mace would do."

"Wait, you met Mace?"

"Yeah, he was the guy who gave me the chips. He won first place. He's really good at cards."

Moby has no clue how close he came to getting himself in real trouble.

Then I have another thought. "Hold on. How the heck did you win second place? You've never even played before!"

"I mean, we watched all those videos. It's not that complicated. It took me a few hands to figure out who was trying to trick me into betting all my chips when they had better cards than me. But once you figure that out, it's not that hard."

I'm stunned. I've always been the brains of this show, or at least I thought I was. Now I know I underestimated the Arch, and I've done the same thing to Moby.

I tell Moby what the Arch told me in the lobby. When I get to the part about the regional tournament, something clicks.

"Did anyone say anything about a regional finals?" I ask.

"Oh, yeah." He fishes in his pocket and pulls out a crumpled piece of paper. "Mace gave me this, too. I can play again tomorrow night if I want."

I smooth out the wad of yellow paper and turn it to catch the light from the parking lot. It's an invitation to play in the regional finals. There's more than enough cash in the envelope to cover the entry fee. The cadre has everything we need to play in the tournament against the Arch.

I secure the envelope in the pocket of my sweatshirt before someone sees us standing around a parking lot with a huge wad of cash. Then a plan starts to take shape in my mind. No great archenemy showdown ever got settled by blackmail. Nobody goes to a movie where the good guy and the bad guy sit down and reason things out in the end. The only way for this kind of thing to be resolved is for one of us to defeat the other in a winner-takes-all confrontation. I have no choice but to use my secret weapon to outmaneuver him once and for all. If my secret weapon is willing to do it, that is.

"So—do you think you could do it again?"

"Do what?"

"You know. Play again, and win?"

"I dunno, it's pretty boring. It's like being in math class with a bunch of adults." Moby starts to walk and I follow.

I consider going through the list of reasons why he needs to say yes. How this is our chance to knock the Arch off his pedestal once and for all. How we finally have the perfect opportunity to make up for all the plots that haven't worked in the past. A million reasons whip around in my head, but in the end I go with the one that really matters. "Could you do it for the cadre?"

He stops and looks at me. "Okay, I'm in."

I let out a relieved breath. "Good. Because I think *you're* the key to taking the Arch down once and for all."

He takes a deep breath and puffs his chest out

with pride. Then his shoulders sink. "I might have TD with the Colonel tomorrow, though." He starts walking again.

I stand there for a minute, then jog to catch up. "Moby, if you pull this off, I will happily do TD for the next year."

"Okay!"

It's too late to tell him I was only joking.

We cross the parking lot toward Madison Street, and Moby slaps the button for a walk signal. He starts hopping from foot to foot. I'd recognize his dookie dance anywhere.

"Gotta go?"

He nods, biting his lip.

"It's not one of your usual times. Are you sure it isn't just gas?"

"I think I was more nervous in there than I thought. Plus, we had curried quinoa for dinner," he says, doubling over.

I have no idea what either of those words means, but I have a brief vision of the Colonel carving a steak as the rest of the family slurps bowls of green slop. "Wanna run back into Thunder Alley?"

"The Clairemont has nice, high toilets and two-ply. I can make it." He winces.

Years of reading his face tell me he has three minutes, tops, before his Dockers become ground zero. It's at least ten minutes to get to the theater.

As the walk signal appears, I nudge him back to the bowling alley.

I understand now why they call it Thunder Alley. There's some sort of bowling league going on, and the crash of bowling balls against pins is deafening. The lights are off on the lanes, replaced by glowing neon stars and a weak, strobing laser that's supposed to make it look like you're bowling in outer space or something. The curry-versus-cheese death match in the men's room will take a while, so I dig into my jeans pockets for the quarters I didn't use earlier and head over to the claw machine to finish what I started.

I pluck at the stuffed kangaroo with the metal claw a few times but only get it to shift a little bit. The tail is now at just the right angle for me to snag it with the claw and make it mine. My hand goes into my pocket, and I mutter a silent prayer for one more quarter.

My prayers are answered. I pull out the coin of destiny and pop it in the slot. The machine comes to life one more time, and I carefully maneuver the claw into position above the prize. This is my last chance to get this right. I check the angles, and I'm just making a few fine-tuning tweaks . . .

"Kangaroo, huh? I was a Kangaroo," says a voice, shattering my nerves.

My thumb flinches on the grab button, and the claw drops, missing the toy by a hair. The guy owes me a quarter, but when I turn around, I don't know what to say.

Standing there in all his pimply-faced glory is the one and only Mace.

CHAPTER 21

Mace and I study each other. He's much shorter than I imagined he'd be from the pictures on the blog.

He looks around to make sure no one is watching, then says, "Here, let me show you the trick."

I step back as he moves toward the machine. He looks around again and then with lightning speed rams his knee into the side of the game, the same way he'll probably do to Archer if he doesn't pay up.

I swallow hard.

The machine comes back to life and the claw resets to its ready position. With a flourish Mace offers me the controls again, but I hesitate and take a step back. I don't want to accept anything he offers.

"Suit yourself," he says, his voice squeaking. "I used to *own* this thing back in the day!"

He steps up to the joystick and gives it a whirl. I have no idea when "the day" was, but his skills have not dulled since then. With the smoothest technique I've ever seen, he guides the claw to the kangaroo, then faces me and says, "Hey, look at me."

I look him in the eye. He winks at me as he pushes the button. He doesn't turn around to watch as the claw lifts the toy out of the pile and drops it in the retrieval slot.

"You go to Alanmoore?" he says.

I nod.

"What? Are you doing the never-talk-to-strangers thing?"

He's much younger than I thought. I suddenly feel bold. "I know who you are, Mace."

He does a double take. "Right, right. I was kind of a legend at Alanmoore. Go, Roos!" he says sarcastically.

"Were you on the track team?"

"You couldn't pay me enough to be on the track team." He laughs. "Besides, do I look like an athlete to you?"

"No, you don't," I say. "So then, what made you such a legend?"

His sunken chest puffs out. "I did all kinds of cool stuff. You ever hear about the time a kid pulled down the principal's pants in front of the whole school and got away with it?"

I run a hand over my scalp. "That's just a school legend."

"Every legend starts somewhere."

I rack my brain for what else I've heard about him. I've got it! "That kid's name was the Fink, not Mace."

"Mason Finklebein." He extends a hand. "Nice to meet you."

I don't offer my hand in return. Am I really face-to-face with the legendary Fink? And if it *is* him, what the heck happened to him since he left Alanmoore?

"If you're such a legend, why'd you change your name?"

He pulls a cigarette from behind his ear and puts it in his mouth but doesn't light it. "I just turned eighteen, I run a different racket now. I have a poker league. Nobody's gonna worry about owing money to *the Fink*, but owing money to a guy named *Mace* . . ." He smashes a fist into his cupped hand, and I jump. "Plus, I've got this leather jacket, so things are going good."

"*Well*," I correct him automatically.

He gives me an odd look. "Well, what?"

"Never mind." I can see why the Arch wants this loser out of his life. I try to think of an excuse to leave. Just then Moby emerges from the men's room sweating like he just did hot yoga. He spots me and hustles over.

When he sees who I'm talking to, he stops in his tracks.

Mace slaps him on the shoulder. "Hey! Winner, winner, chicken dinner. Am I right?"

"It was curried quinoa, actually." Moby takes a step away from him. "I thought you guys didn't know each other."

"We just met," Mace says. "So, you bringing that wad of cash to the regional tomorrow?"

Moby starts to speak, but I jump in before he can give away any of our strategy. "We'll be there."

"Good." Mace nods like a judge considering evidence. "You played good tonight. But we'll see how you do against some real competition."

Moby looks at me, amazed that I'm not correcting Mace's adverb use.

"Yes, we'll see," I say.

Mace claps his hands together. "Well, looks like you and Mustache Man have this all figured out. I will see you boys tomorrow." He turns to walk away. "Good luck getting in," he calls in a taunting voice.

My blood freezes. Of course . . . the fake ID. Mace got one for Archer. He knows we'll need one too. He waves to us over his shoulder. I don't want to ask him for anything, but at this point I don't see a way to get in without his help.

"Fink!" I call.

He stops, shakes his head, then walks back. "Nobody's called me that in five years," he says.

I can't let him intimidate me when I'm this close to finally taking the Arch down. "Can you get us in?"

He tents his fingers and fixes me with a stare. "I do have one ID left, but it'll cost you."

"We need two," I say.

He laughs. "Sorry, shorty, I only have one. Besides, you ain't gonna fool anyone. You want in, you'll have to sneak in."

I pull the envelope of cash out of my pocket and count out enough to pay the entry fee at the regional tournament, plus a few extra bucks, and put it in my pocket. I'll use whatever money is left over in the envelope to buy us a buffet of snacks if we actually get to see *League of Honor* this summer. I want to go into business with this jerk about as much as I want a rash on my butt, but I have to do what I have to do. "How much for the ID?"

Mace takes the envelope with the rest of Moby's winnings in it. *There goes our buffet.* "This should cover it," he says with a wink, and the money disappears into his jacket pocket. From another pocket he pulls out a cell phone and tells Moby to stand against a wall so he can snap pictures for the fake ID.

It's getting late and we need to get to the Clairemont

so Jarek can drive us home. Mace flips through the pictures of Moby on his phone. "These are good. I'll meet you in the coatroom by the lobby of the hotel before the tournament at six twenty."

I don't trust him, but he's our only option. "We'll be there." I push Moby toward the door.

"Hey, kid. You forgot your kangaroo," he calls, holding up the toy from the claw machine.

"Keep it. It means more to you than it does to me."

Thankfully, Jarek lets me use his phone to call the cadre and set up a meeting at the school tomorrow. My dad's car is in the driveway when Jarek drops me off at home.

"Thanks for helping us tonight," I say to Jarek as I hop out.

"No problemo, Mr. Potato Head." He chuckles as he peels away from the curb. He's just messing with me, but the reality of spending the summer thousands of miles away from the nearest decent movie theater opens a pit in my stomach. I close the pit by reminding myself how close I am to finally defeating the Arch.

When I walk in, the front room of the house is empty and all the lights are off. I expect my dad to be in his chair reading the paper. Something is not right. When my eyes adjust, I spot the only sign of life in the house—an odd blue glow coming from the kitchen. I creep through the living room, ready to make a break for it if my parents have been turned into pod people or something, which seems reasonable, since I've never made it this many steps into the house before without being told to do something.

When I get to the kitchen, I stop at the doorway. My parents are speaking Polish, which means they're talking about either money or me.

A board squeaks under my foot, and my father says, "He's here."

My mother calls, "Maciek?"

It's too late to turn back now. Whatever fresh hell (as Stosh would say) they have waiting for me in the kitchen can't be avoided. I put on my fake smile and step into the room. What I see drains all the blood from my head, and the floor falls away beneath my feet. There on the desk in the corner of the kitchen is something I never thought my parents could afford: a beautiful new computer.

Okay, so maybe "beautiful" and "new" are not words I should use to describe the yellowing antique. Two things are obvious—it's gigantic and it comes from a different century. But those are just details. There is an actual computer in my house!

My father sits stooped in front of it. He pokes the keyboard as though he's trying to figure out if it's dead or not. I stand there in shock, staring, wanting to believe one of my dreams has sort of come true.

"It's for homework." My mother smiles at me.

"For business," my father adds. After a few more frustrated jabs at the keyboard, he turns to me. "Do you know how to work it?"

I wait for him to stand, then I sit in front of the beast. "What do you want it to do?"

"Go on the Internet and check your grades," he says.

I roll my eyes, knowing they can't see. "Oooookay." I open the web browser. "Did we get Wi-Fi, too?"

Dad's answer is a stern no.

My mom points a finger up and whispers, "Drones."

My father looks up at the ceiling. "They can listen through walls."

"Riiiight."

My father shows me where the beast is plugged into the wall with a cord. I've always wondered what those little square plugs are for. Apparently, that's where people got their Internet before electricity. For a minute or so the computer makes squealing noises like a bunch of robot cats being stomped to death. When it finally goes silent, the web browser comes up.

"Almost bedtime," my mom says, going to the sink to clean up their dinner dishes.

"I have to go see a man about a horse," my father says, which he thinks is a polite way of telling us he has to take a dump. "When I come back, show me your grades." Leave it to my dad to take all the fun out of the Internet. He stomps out of the kitchen, tucking the newspaper under his arm, which means I have about ten minutes to check Mace's blog and find any updates on the *League of Honor* premiere before he comes back to look at my report card.

I open tabs for Mace's blog and the school's website.

They load super slowly, so I minimize them and open a new tab for the official *League of Honor* page. Nothing has changed since I checked it on Mrs. Belfry's computer a few days ago. I decide to see if Jarek was telling the truth about how long it takes to get movies in Poland. I search "League of Honor" and "Poland," and all I find is an application for a Polish kids' baseball league tryout—not an encouraging sign.

With less than three minutes left I close the other tabs and open Mace's blog. It takes even longer to load than the others. The top banner has barely appeared when the toilet flushes upstairs.

I beg the compusaurus to hurry. "C'mon!" A little more of the page appears, and I can tell the main picture has been changed since last time I looked. Inch by agonizing inch the photo fills in. My blood drops a few degrees as I realize the picture is a full-face shot of tonight's second-place finisher.

Moby's forced smile is barely visible behind the 'stache, but if you look for more than a second, you'll know exactly who it is.

"Is that your school website?" my dad's voice

booms, shaking me out of my state of shock.

I punch the escape key like a jackhammer. The stupid old machine won't respond.

I slap the side of the computer. "It's spam!"

"Poker?" my father says.

My heart almost stops. If he recognizes Moby, I'm getting deported.

"They try to sell you all kinds of weird stuff on the Internet," I say, hoping he won't look too closely.

I reach for the cord and he puts a hand on my shoulder.

"I think it's time for you to go to bed," he says.

"Let me show you how to work this first." I try to buy myself time to flush the page before he sits down to look more closely.

"You go to bed. I see what's going on here." He shoos me out of the chair and sits down in it. He's face-to-face with my best friend, with only a fake mustache keeping us from being discovered. If my dad even senses that we are up to something, he won't let me out of his sight. Our plot to take down the Arch will be ruined, and all the cadre's work will be for nothing.

To top it all off, I'll probably also be sentenced to a summer of hard labor in the old country. I might as well show him how to buy plane tickets online before I go to bed.

As I trudge up the stairs, I hear my mother's voice. "Poker, Kasmir?"

"Don't worry," Dad says. "I know how to keep him away from this kind of bad influence."

CHAPTER 22

Mom and Dad are very quiet over breakfast. The computer sits like an elephant in the corner we all try not to notice. Even though it's switched off, I know it's figuring out a way to betray me. The moment I first saw it, I knew it was too good to be true.

It's not like my dad to keep anything to himself, especially when it comes to disciplining me, so he must be more upset than he's ever been. The thought of what they discovered last night makes my stomach turn. I don't even want to think about how he plans to keep me away from bad influences. Not talking to Moby for a couple of days was pretty tough; I can't imagine not seeing my friends for a whole summer.

After breakfast my parents head out for the shop and leave me a list of chores they think will keep me busy until they get home. As soon as they are gone I fly through the list, doing the absolute minimum so I can say I did them all without lying. Like I requested last night, everyone meets behind the Dumpsters at eleven o'clock to make sure all the pieces of the plan are in place.

"Shelby, did you talk to Sam?" I ask.

"Yes, the student council meets on Monday. That's when the treasurer, Sherman, will give Archer the check from the activities treasury to buy the uniforms," she says.

"Which he will actually use to pay back Mace?" one McQueen asks.

I touch my fingertips together. "If things go according to plan, Mace will never get his hands on the school's money."

The hatted McQueen says, "Why are you trying to beat him at poker? Why not just turn him in?"

"He hasn't taken any money from the school yet,

so there isn't anything to turn him in for except playing poker," I say. "Trust me, I know his mom and dad. His punishment would be a slap on the wrist. If he wins enough at the regional to pay off Mace, he gets to give the club money back and tell everyone *he* got new uniforms donated."

"If that happens, he'll look like even more of a hero than he already does," Sizzler says.

"Exactly," I say. "That can't happen. We need him to lose the tournament, so he has to take the club money to pay back Mace. Once he does that, we have him where we want him."

"We see," says the McQueen, even though I suspect he doesn't. "And how exactly do we make sure he doesn't win enough to pay this Mace back?"

"We've got a man on the inside." I put my hand on Moby's shoulder. Or at least we will if Mace comes through on his end of the deal and gets us the fake ID.

The regional tournament is being held in the ballroom of a fancy hotel downtown. On the drive home last night I worked out a deal with Jarek to drive us

Saturday night and cover for us with my parents. In return I have to sweep up the Clairemont all summer (assuming I'm still in the United States), throw in some of my best comic books, and do "a favor to be named later." It's a steep cost, but bringing down the Arch's scheme is worth almost any price.

There's a track meet that afternoon, so Sizzler is assigned to keep his eye on the Arch. Ever since he escorted Sherman to our little meeting, it hasn't been a secret that he's in the cadre. The Arch won't talk to him, but he's still on the track team. Moby, Shelby, and I spend the afternoon at my house, since my parents are at the shop. We try to watch TV, but nerves make it impossible to concentrate. Sizzler calls us to keep us informed about the Arch's whereabouts. Apparently, the stress of leading multiple lives is wearing on the Arch, because according to Sizzler, he doesn't win any of the races that day.

I fidget with the computer, trying unsuccessfully to make it move faster. Shelby uses her theater skills to apply Moby's mustache and wig while he finally finishes *Watchmen*. It's a pretty complicated story about a bunch of superheroes and villains that doesn't end the way you expect a comic to end. The good guys don't save the day.

"So that's it? The bad guy wins!" He slaps the cover shut.

"Yes and no. See, *he* doesn't think he's the bad guy." I don't try to explain it any more than that. It's one of those things you just have to think about for a while.

Jarek shows up right when my parents get home from work. He makes a big deal out of us being late so my parents won't have time to ask questions. The commotion keeps them distracted while Moby and Shelby sneak out my window. The last thing we need is my parents asking why there was a girl in the house and why Moby looks like a police officer from 1976.

Moby is already in the backseat when we get to the car. I breathe a sigh of relief when we buckle in and pull away from the house.

"I hope you guys know what you're doing," Jarek says, weaving through traffic.

Moby tilts forward from the backseat. The sight of the mustache glued to his face makes my cousin flinch.

"Don't worry, we've done this before." Moby leans back, yanking his dad's suit out of his backpack.

Jarek just shakes his head and smashes the gas pedal to the floor.

He drops us off a block away from the hotel so we won't risk being spotted by someone we know. We find the side entrance to the lobby that Mace told us about and go in. We slink around the edge of the room. A gigantic potted plant serves as cover while we take in the lay of the place. Across the lobby we spot the coatroom where we're supposed to meet Mace.

"There it is," Moby says.

There are tons of people in the lobby. Any one of them might know my parents. I whisper, "We need to find a way around all these people." He doesn't answer, and when I turn to tell him again, I see why.

He's gone.

I scan the lobby and catch a glimpse of a wrinkled gray suit weaving its way to the coatroom. I pull my sweatshirt hood over my head, spring from my hiding spot, and catch up to him.

There's no sign of Mace. The coatroom is empty.

I guess I should've expected as much. What can I do now? Tell on him for taking Moby's gambling winnings and not giving us the fake ID he promised?

We wait five minutes past the time we were supposed to meet before I decide we should go look for Mace.

"C'mon, Mobe. . . ." The smell of leather and cigarettes hits me half a second before I bump into Mace.

He acts as surprised as we are. "Whoa! Where's the fire, Lex Luthor?"

"You're late," I say.

"And you are ungrateful," he says with a smirk.

"I already paid you. Remember? You were supposed to be here five minutes ago. We're on a schedule."

He raises an eyebrow. "All right. That's the spirit." He fumbles in his pockets. "I asked around about you, you know. You've got kind of a reputation."

A few beads of perspiration soak into my hood. I don't like the idea of this guy knowing anything about me.

"I hear you've picked up the torch."

Moby comes to my defense. "It wasn't a torch, it was a lighter. And Archer lit—"

"What is that supposed to mean?" I cut Moby off.

Mace pulls out the ID card, looks at it, grins, and flicks it with his finger. "You know, messing with the jocks. Sounds like you got that old museum of a school wired. I'm glad someone's carrying on the traditions I started."

Does he really think that he and I are somehow the same? That my anti-Arch activities are me picking up the torch? The thought of it makes a metallic taste rise in the back of my throat. The coatroom now feels half the size it did when we walked in, and it's getting smaller all the time. I want to tell him that he and I are nothing alike, and I plan on dropping the torch just as soon as I take out the Arch. But he doesn't deserve to hear it. I need to get out of here and away from this guy.

I hold out my hand and Mace gives me the card. I have to admit, it looks like a real driver's license—or at least what I imagine a driver's license from Arizona must look like. I'm twice as sure about our chances than I was ten minutes ago. I hand the card to Moby.

"You *boys* have fun tonight," Mace says with a chuckle.

"Thanks. We will," Moby says, spoiling my chance to stare Mace down as he leaves the room.

I turn to Moby. "You ready to do this?"

"I'm nervous, Chub."

"About what?"

"What if someone recognizes me?"

His wig and mustache look good. I smooth out the bigger creases in the suit. "Nobody will recognize you," I say, wishing I believed it as much as I sound like I do.

"All right, I'm ready."

Back in the lobby Moby spots a digital reader board that says the regional finals are in the Grand Ballroom, one floor below the lobby. A flood of people head for the stairs. We wait until no one is watching, then slide into the crowd and make our way downstairs.

When I see the check-in counter, it's clear we aren't at Thunder Alley anymore. The security here is much more serious. The guys checking everyone in are even wearing earpieces like the Secret Service.

Moby has an ID, but I don't. I'm counting on

one of the McQueens' famous diversions to give me a chance to sneak in too. I will need to time things perfectly to be at the front of the line when they do whatever it is they have planned at 6:35.

We spot the players' entrance, and I check the clock on the wall. We watch for a few minutes to see how quickly they are letting people in. They're averaging three players a minute. At exactly 6:33 we step into the line behind six other players. I draw the string of my hood tight and keep my head down as we wait for our turn. If the McQueens are ever going to come through for the cadre, now is the time.

The line moves quickly, and it's only 6:34 when we get to the front. We'll have to stall.

The guard holds out a hand the size of a bunch of bananas. "Invitation and ID," he says.

"Yup," Moby says, staring at the ground.

"May I see it, Mr. . . . ?"

Moby doesn't answer, so I kick him in the foot.

"Oh, right," he says. He pulls the invite and the new ID from his pocket and practically throws them at the guard.

As the guard studies the ID card, my heart almost stops. He raises one eyebrow, then the other. This is it—my greatest plot ever is over before it begins.

Then his look dissolves into a smile, which he tries to hide. With tight lines stretched at the corners of his mouth, he says, “Chi Chi Montana?”

Moby just looks at the ground. I kick him again.

“He’s hard of hearing,” I say a little too loudly. “Aren’t you, Chi Chi?”

He looks at the guard. I pray he will just say a simple yes so we can go in.

This time my prayers are not answered.

Moby points to his ear. “Sorry, army.”

The guard straightens up but still looks suspicious. “Where did you serve?”

My head is a fountain of sweat now.

“Well . . .” Moby takes a deep breath. He’s about to improvise. I cough loudly into my hand. Thankfully, he takes the hint. “It’s classified.”

The guard looks at the ID one more time, then hands it back to Moby.

“And you are?” he says to me.

"He's my son?" Moby says, just as the clock on the wall flips to 6:35.

The guard's forehead wrinkles. "Oookay, I'm going to need to see your ID too, sir."

Anytime now. What is taking the McQueen Special so long?

"Your ID, sir?" He folds his hands in front of him and lets out an impatient sigh.

I make a big show out of checking my pockets.

"Did you look in your wallet?" Moby suggests. I shoot him a look to let him know he isn't helping. He just shakes his head and shrugs at the guard. "Kids."

The man nods and starts to say, "Mmm-hmm," but he's cut off by a deep boom from somewhere in the hotel. The crystal in the chandeliers tinkles together, and the lights blink for a second. People look around and murmur as security guards press their earpieces into their ears. I glance at the clock as the guard who was checking us in rushes from his post.

The McQueens have come through again.

CHAPTER 23

The McQueens' diversion creates enough chaos for me to sneak through the door behind Moby. We press into the crowded ballroom and don't look back. At the center of the ballroom are the green felt tables where the matches will be played. Bleachers surround the tables on three sides, creating a mini-stadium for the spectators. This is definitely a bigger deal than the games Mace runs in the basement of the bowling alley.

I lead Moby to a dark corner behind a set of bleachers, scanning the room for the Arch as we go. We still have twenty minutes until the games start, and I need to make sure there will be no surprises.

"Are you ready for this?" I ask.

Moby nods. He tries to stand tall and look confident, but I catch the rotten-vegetable smell of the fart he just sneaked out.

I fan the air.

"Sorry."

I fight back a gag. "It's okay. The cadre is counting on you." I clap a hand on his shoulder, and he straightens up again. "Do you remember the plan?"

"Don't . . . win," he recites.

"Don't win, buuuut . . ."

"Buuuut . . . don't let the Arch win either."

"Perfect."

"It would be a lot easier if I could just win, though."

I can't have him changing the plan at this point. "We've talked about this, Mobe. First and second place are the two spots that win money. We just have to make sure Archer isn't one of them."

Moby shifts from foot to foot. "But I think I can win it!"

"Look around you," I say. "The guy who won this

tournament last year is on TV all the time now. Do you think we'll get away with this if you have to do an interview after it's over?"

His eyes flick back to mine.

"Do you know who won second place last year?"

"No."

"Good, neither do I. All we need to do is keep the Arch out of the top two, and his reign as resident superhero of Alanmoore Middle School is over." *And Archer will finally pay for what he did to me.*

The farthest set of bleachers is filling up. The top row is deep in the shadows, just like the bleachers in our gym. I'm about to go grab a seat when I see a very familiar face.

Mr. Mayer makes his way up the stairs and sits right in the spot I wanted. There are two more sets of bleachers, so I decide to find someplace where I won't be sitting directly across from him.

Just then there's a commotion by the players' entrance. I stand on my tiptoes to see what's going on. The small crowd parts to make room for a guy in a black felt cowboy hat with a silly blue feather in the band.

Mr. X is in the house.

A security guard walks by, talking into a walkie-talkie. "Cherry bomb in the toilet?" the guard says, grinning the grin of a former troublemaker. "It knocked it clean off the wall? *Classic!*"

That explains the boom. Apparently, the McQueens have graduated from newspapers and soup.

I need to take my spot before somebody else does, so I slip around the back of the bleachers and up the stairs into the shadows. From my seat I watch as the Arch shakes hands with Mace. As he tries to let go, Mace pulls him in close and whispers something in his ear. The brim of the cowboy hat shadows the Arch's face, his body tenses, and he leans away. Mace is probably reminding him what will happen if he doesn't pay back the money he owes.

I remember Mace forcing the claw machine to do his bidding with a quick jab of his knee. I wince imagining the Arch on the receiving end of that shot. It should make me happy to see my nemesis with his tail between his legs, but ever since we confronted each other at Thunder Alley, I'm having a hard time despising him. Since then I've caught myself thinking of him more as the kid who used to be my best friend, instead of the fake hero he's been posing as. Watching Mace intimidate him now reminds me that even though he's taller than I'll ever be, he's still just a kid tangled up in a dangerous adult game.

Besides, he was never Mace's best friend. When the Arch finally faces the music for all of this, I don't want it to be at the hands of some overgrown bully. I want him to live the rest of his life knowing it was the friend he tried to forget that took him down.

The lights dim and everyone goes quiet as a man in a suit walks out in front of the crowd. "Ladies and gentlemen, welcome to the regional finals of the Great Northwest Poker League. Let's meet the players!"

The lights blaze back to life, revealing the players seated at six tables. The crowd ripples with applause.

"Tonight's format will be blah . . . blah . . . blah . . ." The announcer explains the rules, and the dealers start passing out cards. It's hard to tell exactly what's going on, but by watching the players' body language and the size of their stacks of chips, it's pretty obvious who the winners and losers are. *I wonder what my parents would think if they saw all of this money being thrown away on a game.*

I draw my hood even tighter, making the hole just big enough for me to keep one eye on Mr. Mayer and one on Moby.

After an hour and a half of watching players get eliminated, my butt is numb and my legs are asleep. They started with six tables but are down to just one. The remaining seven players are seated at the final table. Moby is at one end, the Arch at the other. Mace is in the middle position, across from the dealer.

Cheating must not be the only way Mace can win. He has to have some sort of skill to have made it to the last table at a legitimate tournament. Mace has the largest pile of chips, Archer's is half the size of Mace's, and Moby's is smaller still. It isn't time to panic yet. Moby is still in it, and Mace can't cheat here.

I have to believe Moby can do it.

Stacks of chips grow and shrink, and one by one players leave the table shaking their heads, until finally just the Arch, Mace, and Moby are left.

For the plan to work, the Arch has to walk out empty-handed. It's all up to Moby now.

The room goes quiet as the dealer hands each player two cards and the players study them. Then all three players toss chips into the middle. This is the first bet they all have to make if they want to see the next three cards.

The dealer will flip three of the five cards in front of her, and then the players get to mix her cards with the two secret ones they are holding. If they think their combination is good enough to beat everyone else's, they'll stay in and try to get the other players to bet all their money so they can take it.

Moby sinks in his chair little by little as the dealer flips each new card. His shoulders sag almost to the floor when she turns over the third one. I can't be sure from this far away, but it looks like he might cry. I can't blame him. If there's one thing I've learned, it's that sometimes you can do everything right and still get dealt the wrong cards. He's given it his best effort for the cadre and he's come up a little short.

The dealer motions to Moby. He taps the table and in his fake deep voice says, "Check." It means he wants to see what the other guys do before he bets. I think he's stalling because he knows it's over.

A sharky grin is plastered across the Arch's face. He sees the same thing in Moby's body language that I do—his cards aren't good enough to win. The Arch licks his lips, probably tasting the victory that's just one bet away.

Mace bets next. He frowns at his cards too, but he has enough chips that he doesn't have to worry about losing them all this hand. He counts out the same amount of chips from his own pile that the Arch has in his and pushes them to the center of the table. Then he slouches back in his chair and waits to see if his bet will pay off. If the Arch wants to stay in the game, he needs to push his entire pile into the middle of the table.

The Arch has done the math just like I have. With Moby about to lose, second place is guaranteed. Without a moment's hesitation the Arch shoves his entire pile of chips into the center, and the crowd lets out a gasp.

"All in," someone next to me whispers. When the Arch wins this hand, he will have enough chips to sit back and wait for a great hand to take Moby out. After he wins this hand, it will be over.

Moby's hunched over, his suit even more wrinkled than it already was. I wish I could go stand by him right now, but I can't.

The Arch leans forward, folds his arms on the table, and glares a challenge at Moby. Every eye in the place is on Moby, waiting to see what he will do. He flips some of his chips back and forth on the felt.

"C'mon, Moby!" I say under my breath, hoping against hope there is some way to rescue this.

The entire room waits to see what he will do. The Arch and Mace both sit taller.

When it's clear Moby isn't going to act without prodding, the dealer says, "Your bet, sir."

Moby shakes his head in defeat. The Arch lets out a cocky chuckle as he waits for his plot to work out just like he planned.

I suspect Moby is trying to figure out a way to pull one of his famous escapes in front of a ballroom full of people, when he looks up at the dealer. "Huh?"

The Arch snorts and Mace rolls his eyes.

The dealer sighs. "Your bet, Mr. Montana."

Mace chimes in, "Yeah, *Chi Chi*. What have you got?"

Suddenly Moby sits up straight in his chair, the defeated posture gone.

The Arch shifts nervously in his seat. All of his chips are already in the pot.

"Go, Roos," Moby says, winking at the Arch.

The confidence flushes from the Arch's face as he suddenly realizes who Chi Chi Montana actually is.

What the heck is happening? Is this the moment I've been dreaming about since second grade?

The Arch looks like he's been kicked in the nuts as Moby shoves all of his chips into the middle of the table.

"It's called a bluff!" Moby says. We're under the bleachers now that it's all over.

I'm still trying to understand what he's just done. "You tricked him into betting it all and losing!"

"That was the plan, right?" he says.

I shake my head. "That was *exactly* the plan!"

Moby holds up the second-place prize, a gaudy gold-plated bracelet, admiring it like a new species of frog he's just discovered. "I've never won anything before."

I don't want to crush his moment, so I let him admire his prize. "You know, Mobe, no one can ever know about that thing."

"*You* know," he says, flipping it into a trash can and pulling out an envelope of prize money. "Check this out." He hands it to me. It's a lot heavier than the last one, and my eyes bulge at the sight of all those hundred-dollar bills.

We wait under the bleachers while Mace collects his winnings and talks to a reporter. The place is deserted when he finally walks by us. Moby and I step out of the shadows and block his way.

He nods at Moby. "Nice play, guy. Too bad it was only good for second place."

"That's okay. I lost on purpose," Moby says matter-of-factly.

Mace raises an eyebrow, unable to comprehend why someone would do that.

"It's a long story," Moby says.

"Make sure you bring that prize money to my next game," Mace says with a wink.

"Yeah, that won't be happening," I say, pulling out the envelope and flipping through the bills. "In fact, the money is kind of what I want to talk to you about."

CHAPTER 24

I'm at school early on Monday to get to the Arch before he has a chance to do anything. I hide in a hollow between two banks of lockers and wait. When the Arch opens his locker, I run over and stand behind the open door to do that cool thing where he shuts the door and I'm all of a sudden standing there. I smile when he jumps at the sight of me.

His eyes are red and puffy like a pair of meatballs. He clearly hasn't slept since the tournament, probably wondering when Mace would come to collect what he's owed.

"What do you want?" he sneers.

"I hear track isn't panning out, so I wanted to invite you to drama club."

"What's that supposed to mean?"

I take a step closer to him. Being seen with me in the halls makes him uncomfortable, and I still want him to squirm a little bit. "It means today's the day you vote to give the money back to the clubs, tell everyone about the donated uniforms, and stop pretending to be something you're not."

"It's not that simple." He leans his head against his locker.

"I think it's exactly that simple. It's time you stopped pretending to be who people expect you to be, Archer. You actually aren't that good at it."

"That's not what I mean. I owe Mace a ton of money. I could've beaten him in a straight-up game and paid him off, but you and your little minion screwed it all up." He shakes his head. "Now I'm in bigger trouble than ever."

He knows there are no more moves he can make. The game is over and he lost.

Who has checkmate now?

The Arch whispers something under his breath.

"What was that?" I say.

He head-butts his locker and kicks the door. "I said . . . I'm sorry."

"You will be when Mace gets ahold of you. He—"

He cuts me off. "Not for that."

"What, then?"

He rubs his eyes hard with one hand, then jams it back into his pocket. "I wish I'd never walked out of the basement that day. None of this would've happened if . . . I guess I just wish we'd never stopped being friends."

I'm stunned by the words he just said. This is all I ever wanted to hear but absolutely the last thing I expected him to say to my face. We stand in silence for a minute or more. I think we're both afraid to speak.

"Why did you walk out on me like that?" I say.

He wipes his nose on his sleeve. "I don't know. I guess I panicked when I saw what happened to your hair. Then the next day you went from being just some kid to being the kid who gave the whole school lice. I saw how everyone looked at you, and I knew I couldn't take them looking at me the same way. After that there was no going back."

"Things don't have to be the way they've been," I say. "It's up to us."

"Your hair isn't going to grow back."

My scalp gets warm and I run a hand over it.

"Everybody thinks I'm *the Arch*. There's nothing I can do about it anymore."

I shake my head.

The truth is I'm tired of fighting with the Arch. And if the path I've been on ends with me running a crooked poker league in the basement of a bowling alley? Count me out.

If my dad decides to sentence me to hard labor, so be it. I'll dig those potatoes. Then I'll come home and watch *League of Honor* on the Colonel's Blu-ray player and go back to school next year as a normal student with his very own cadre.

The Arch twists on the hook long enough. I fish in my pocket and pull out a handwritten note.

"Call another vote today. Fund the clubs," I say.

"But Mace will kill me."

I hand him the note.

"What's this?" He unfolds the piece of paper and reads. "Who's . . . Mason Finklebein?"

"That's a receipt from Mace showing your debt to him is paid in full."

I watch as it slowly sinks in what he's holding.

He stares at the note in disbelief. "You paid my debt to Mace?"

"Welllll, technically Moby did, since it was his money. Consider it a gift from the cadre."

"The who?"

"Never mind." I still have some business to clear up before the first bell, and I need to get going. "You're out. It's over." Then I turn and walk away.

"Thank you," he says in a small voice.

I stop and turn back around. "You can thank me by doing the right thing when you meet today." I want it to be the last word, but I can tell he has something else on his mind.

He finally looks me in the eye. "I don't know if I can stop being him."

I think about it for a second. "The Arch isn't much without a nemesis," I say. "So if you want to keep pretending to be some sort of hero, you'll have to find somebody else to play the villain."

I walk away knowing the cadre and I have done the last thing anyone would've expected a bunch of outcasts to do. We've helped our enemy when he needed it most. Hopefully, in the process, we've put out the light known as the Arch.

I know I'm done living in the shadows.

Mrs. Osborne can't hide her surprise when I ask to see Mr. Mayer. Usually when I end up in the office, he's already expecting me. As the Colonel would say, he looks like a can of smashed buttholes when I walk into his office.

I hand him the envelope with his own note from Mace, then walk out without saying a word.

I have one more envelope in my pocket and only a few minutes until the first bell. I go outside to where the janitor's office is and slip the last envelope under the door. After the debts were paid, lots of money was left over. The cadre agreed it would be best used to buy a new kangaroo costume so Mr. Kraley doesn't have to put on the purple-stained BO suit anymore. The guy has been through enough already. I hope he's happy when he opens the envelope and sees the receipt for the new one that an anonymous athletic supporter ordered for him.

Maybe I've had a little growth spurt while I've been busy plotting against the Arch, or maybe it's the fact that the weight of the world is off my shoulders, but I swear I feel a few inches taller as I walk out from between the Dumpsters today. I stop in the parking lot and fill my lungs with air. The old school doesn't look as menacing now that I'm enemy-free.

For the first time I can remember, I push open the doors excited about what waits for me inside.

I find Moby in the hall, looking lost as usual. He probably doesn't remember me telling him I would meet him at school instead of the regular spot. He has a pained look on his face, which I immediately recognize. He's missed his morning sit-down.

"Hey, Mobe," I say.

"Hey, Chub. I was looking all over for you. Where were you?"

"I was taking care of all the stuff we talked about yesterday," I explain.

"Oh, right." He winces.

"Did you miss your toilet session?"

He nods glumly.

"You can probably—" The first bell rings and a tide of kids start toward their homerooms. There isn't time before the final bell to release a mud weasel back into the wild.

We climb the stairs to Mr. Funk's room. When we get there, everyone is already sitting down. The spokes-McQueen tips the hat in salute and the other two nod. Shelby and Sizzler have saved two seats for Moby and me.

Shelby leans forward. "How did it go?"

I shrug. It's out of my hands now. "I guess we'll find out after their meeting."

The McQueens lounge in their seats, radiating pride over Saturday's events.

"Cherry bombs in the toilet?" I ask.

The hat gives me a gleeful grin. "We always wanted to try it. Worked, didn't it?" The other two smile like hyenas.

Mr. Funk comes into the room as the bell rings, and dumps his usual armload of papers on his desk. "All right. Everybody calm down," he says, even though no one is even talking.

Then a sound pierces the silence. It starts like a high note on a violin. After a few seconds it becomes a cello, and after a few more seconds it morphs into a sound like a trumpet being played by someone who's getting punched in the stomach. By the time the sound of the blast fades, the whole classroom, including the teacher, is staring at Moby and me.

Someone at the front of the room calls, "Sweet fancy Moses," which gets a laugh or two.

Then someone yells, "Who cut the cheese?" and everyone laughs.

I look at Moby. He's about to raise his hand and admit to the fart.

Before he can, I shoot my hand into the air first and yell, "It was me!"

Some more kids start laughing. I scan their faces, looking as many of them straight in the eye as I can. Most of them stop laughing when my eyes meet theirs.

Then the giggling stops completely and the classroom goes silent.

I breathe through my mouth to avoid gagging as I keep my hand proudly in the air. When I turn back around to reassure Moby, I see why the room is quiet.

The entire cadre—my cadre—has their hands in the air too.

ACKNOWLEDGMENTS

Most people think writers work alone.

Most people couldn't be more wrong.

This book owes its life to many people.

First I want to thank the most amazing adopted family anyone could ask for, my critique group, the Papercuts. Angie, Cindy, David, Donna, Jason, Kayla: Without each of your honest (and occasionally brutal) critiques, Chub would not exist. I love you guys even more than I love bacon pancakes.

Melissa Koosman, not only were you one of the first to take a scalpel to this manuscript, but you introduced me to the love of my life as well. I owe you more than I can ever repay, so let's just call it even?

My agent, the indefatigable Sarah Davies. You took me in and showed me the way. You are my Yoda. Hopefully, we can travel a long way in this canoe.

Marissa Graff, you helped me polish this turd before we sent it out on submission. You've become a great friend. I hear your voice in my ear every time I touch the keyboard.

My editor, Amy Cloud. You got what I was going for from the beginning. I couldn't have asked for a better person to guide me through my first work adventure into the world of publishing. You have been an absolute dream to work with. Thank you for giving *Fartacus* a home at Aladdin.

Rob, you remind me every day that I'm a writer. I couldn't have done this without you gently cattle-prodding me along.

My fourth-grade teacher, Mr. Tivnan. You introduced me to Bilbo, Smaug, and company, and showed me that you don't hae to be a kid to think stories are awesome.

G-Money. Thank you for making sure I didn't embarrass myself in the card game scenes.

My dad, for being the best example I ever had.

I want to thank everyone at SCBWI Western Washington and the Pacific Northwest Writer's Association for helping me make the connections that ultimately turned my dream of being an author into a reality.

The thing that makes any of this worth doing is

my family. My first readers, Bethany and Sophia, you let me know when my jokes didn't quite land the way I'd hoped. Max and Elena, you guys didn't directly impede my progress; thanks for that, I guess.

My amazing partner in writing and in life, Donna, you help me every day to become not only a better writer, but a better man as well. This book wouldn't exist if it weren't for you. Thank you for sharing this experience with me. I love you.

I also want to thank my publisher, Mara Anastas, and all the people at Aladdin who made this book happen. Cover illustrator Dan Widdowson, designer Laura Lyn DiSiena, production editor Kerry Johnson, copy editor Erica Stahler, the marketing team of Tara Grieco and Carolyn Swerdloff, the fantastic sales force, and countless others who've done the real work of bringing *Fartacus* into the world.

Finally, I need to thank God for all the blessings I've been given. Seeing my name on a real live book is at the very top of the list.